Blood ma

There was pandemonium and confusion everywhere I looked. Women screamed. Children cried out in pain and fear.

I looked around for a weapon so I could defend myself. I found a lance and picked it up. The minute I had it in my hands, one of the marauders charged straight at me.

When he came within a few yards of me, I drew back my arm and hurled the lance . . . striking the warrior in the stomach. Blood gushed from his body. There was a surprised look in his eyes. I stood there, frozen, as he squirmed.

I began to tremble all over. I had killed a man. With my own hands, I had taken a human life.

Berkley titles by Jory Sherman

THE VIGILANTE
THE VIGILANTE: SIX-GUN LAW

THE DARK LAND
SUNSET RIDER
TEXAS DUST
BLOOD RIVER
THE SAVAGE GUN
THE SUNDOWN MAN

The Sundown Man

JORY SHERMAN

BERKLEY BOOKS, NEW YORK

THE BERKLEY PUBLISHING GROUP
Published by the Penguin Group
Penguin Group (USA) Inc.
375 Hudson Street, New York, New York 10014, USA
Penguin Group (Canada), 90 Eglinton Avenue East, Suite 700, Toronto, Ontario M4P 2Y3, Canada
(a division of Pearson Penguin Canada Inc.)
Penguin Books Ltd., 80 Strand, London WC2R 0RL, England
Penguin Group Ireland, 25 St. Stephen's Green, Dublin 2, Ireland (a division of Penguin Books Ltd.)
Penguin Group (Australia), 250 Camberwell Road, Camberwell, Victoria 3124, Australia
(a division of Pearson Australia Group Pty. Ltd.)
Penguin Books India Pvt. Ltd., 11 Community Centre, Panchsheel Park, New Delhi—110 017, India
Penguin Group (NZ), 67 Apollo Drive, Rosedale, North Shore 0745, Auckland, New Zealand
(a division of Pearson New Zealand Ltd.)
Penguin Books (South Africa) (Pty.) Ltd., 24 Sturdee Avenue, Rosebank, Johannesburg 2196,
South Africa

Penguin Books Ltd., Registered Offices: 80 Strand, London WC2R 0RL, England

This is a work of fiction. Names, characters, places, and incidents either are the product of the author's imagination or are used fictitiously, and any resemblance to actual persons, living or dead, business establishments, events, or locales is entirely coincidental.

THE SUNDOWN MAN

A Berkley Book / published by arrangement with the author

PRINTING HISTORY
Berkley edition / July 2007

Copyright © 2007 by Jory Sherman.
Cover illustration by Bruce Emmett.
Cover design by Steven Ferlauto.

ISBN: 978-0-425-21630-9

BERKLEY®
Berkley Books are published by The Berkley Publishing Group,
a division of Penguin Group (USA) Inc.,
375 Hudson Street, New York, New York 10014.
BERKLEY is a registered trademark of Penguin Group (USA) Inc.
The "B" design is a trademark belonging to Penguin Group (USA) Inc.

PRINTED IN THE UNITED STATES OF AMERICA

10 9 8 7 6 5 4 3 2 1

For Leslie King

One

I am the story, much as I hate to be, but that's just the way it is. I am the story because of all the things that happened to me so long ago and how I came to be who I am today. But a story isn't just one person and what happened didn't just happen to me. It happened to my family, and most of them can't be the story because they can't tell it. That's why I'm the story and why I have to tell it just the way it all happened.

Even now, telling it, I feel like I'm staring straight down the business end of a gun, and at someone I don't even know who has his finger on the trigger, squeezing it so slow my insides turn to mush.

Oh, the horror of it. The horror of that day, that last day of my father's life, and my mother's, and a cloudless blue sky so serene and beautiful, and the blood, their blood, soaking into the prairie, their lives leaking away just moments after they were alive, their muscles working, their legs walking, their voices raised in alarm.

The horror lingers, and it's difficult for me to discuss those last moments when my world, and my sister's, was shattered, scattered, decimated like broken pottery, and I hesitate to begin reassembling the events of that day, which, for so long, seemed a blur, a cacophony of images shrieking in my brain as if a series of paintings on a wall had the ability to scream.

My name is Jared Sunnedon, a Finnish name, according to my father. Over time, after my family came to this country, the "e" became silent, so people never heard it right when I said it, so they started calling me "Sundown," and later after I gained an unsavory reputation as a gunfighter, they called me "The Sundown Man." I hated the appellation, but I had to admit it saved time when I was in a tight spot, and I was in a number of those the past few years. Sometimes, a reputation can give the bearer a bit of an edge.

I never thought of any of these things when we set out from Kansas City in the spring of 1874. My pa had joined up with a small wagon train heading for Oregon, and Ma had our wagon filled with supplies for the journey and some of her precious belongings, including a small spinet piano, a modest chest of drawers, clothing, and such. I had my books, and Kate, my kid sister, had her dulcimer and dolls. Pa had his printing press, of course. He wanted to set up a newspaper somewhere in Oregon. He was a pretty good reporter and wanted to be on his own.

The wagon boss was a mean bastard named Cassius Hogg, but like many such folks, he hid his true nature from all of us. None of us suspected that he was a vicious, heartless man, with a streak of greed in him as wide as a barn door. There were two other families of pilgrims who had signed up with Hogg. One was David Prentiss, a storekeeper; his wife, Sally; and their daughter, Violet, who was about sixteen at the time. The other gullible family was a carpenter feller name of Giacomo Bandini, a Venetian from Italy; his wife, Francesca; and their twin sons, eight years old, Mario and Matteo, handsome, dark-eyed, dark-haired urchins who looked like little scrubbed angels in the fancy Little Lord Fauntleroy clothes they wore on the first day out. They weren't so clean-faced, nor dressed so well, after that first week across the Kansas prairie.

Every day, we traveled from sunrise until nearly sunset, but one day we stopped early in the afternoon so everyone, including the animals, could get some well-deserved rest.

That's when we found out that Hogg was carrying two boxes of brand-new Winchester rifles in Mr. Prentiss's wagon. When Hogg asked if we wanted to hunt antelope with him, he took out one of the boxes and showed us the new rifles. He handed one to my father.

My father reached for the rifle when Hogg handed it toward him. Hogg let go of it too soon and my father grabbed for it. The rifle slipped from his grasp and struck the wagon. My father lunged for it and slammed it up against the boards. The rifle slipped down across an exposed nail. When he finally grasped it and held it up, I saw that there was a scratch in the new barrel. It looked like a small silver scar.

"Damn you, Sven Sunnedon," Hogg yelled. "That there Winchester's brand-spankin'-new."

"Sorry," Pa said.

"I ought to make you buy it, but I got other plans for these here '73s."

"As long as you don't shoot me with it," Pa said.

"I've a good mind to." Hogg turned and walked away.

After that, nothing more was said about the slightly damaged rifle and we left early the following morning.

The first couple of weeks were fun for us young kids. I was the oldest, almost seventeen, and Kate was but fourteen. She played with her dolls and I read my books, *Ivanhoe*, *The Count of Monte Cristo*, and works by Homer, among others. At night, Ma would read some from the Bible, and she'd play the spinet while Kate plunked her dulcimer, and we'd sing the simple songs. The singing seemed to irritate Hogg, but he had not yet shown his true colors and none us of suspected what a black heart he had beating inside that big barrel chest of his.

Until we got well into the Territory of Colorado, a vast, endless prairie with snowcapped peaks in the hazy distance. We were all pretty excited, and some of us rode bareback out in front of the wagons to get a better look at those beautiful mountains bathed in a purple haze. Hogg had already ridden off, saying he was going to do some scouting. He mumbled something about "Rappyhoe," and we didn't know what he meant.

Kate and I rode over a small rise and saw a dip in the trail that opened up onto a vast landscape of high grass and a wonderland of buttes and mesas that seemed to suck all the breath out of our lungs. It was then that we saw some young brown-skinned boys lying on their backs atop a little knoll. They were working their bare legs like scissors, and that's when we saw some antelope coming toward them, one in the lead, about four others several yards behind them. Beyond those pronghorns was a larger herd. We already knew what they were because we had seen many of them after we got into the Territory of Colorado and left Kansas behind. In fact, Hogg had shot one and had his cook prepare it one night. It tasted, he said, like goat meat, but I had never eaten goat, so I just shrugged and ate it. The meat was tough and stringy, but it satisfied my hunger that night.

Kate was excited and pulled on my sleeve.

"Let's ride down to where those boys are," she said. "Ask them why they're doing such a foolish thing."

"I think they're hunting," I said. "Those antelope are mighty curious. Look, those boys have bows next to them and each one has an arrow in it. See, those are their quivers alongside. Those are red Indians, Kate, and we don't want to fool with them."

"How do you know those boys are hunting?" she asked.

"'Cause that was just the way Hogg and his men did it when they shot that antelope a few days ago."

"You went with them?"

"I followed them."

She looked at me right sharp as if I'd just revealed a secret side of myself, which I had. I wanted to know what was going on in the world.

Right after that, we saw Hogg and one of his drovers, a man named Rudy Truitt, both of them all hunched over, carrying rifles, come sneaking up on those Indian boys from two different directions, like arrows shot from bows. I opened my mouth to shout out a warning, but my voice froze in my throat as if my neck was clamped tight by an icy hand.

Hogg and Truitt rode right up and shot those two boys with their Winchesters. I heard two cracks and saw the boys twitch and then stiffen up. They were plumb dead, I knew. Hogg and Truitt jumped down from their horses and ran up to the dead Indians and drew their knives. They knelt down and cut the braids where they joined the skulls and held up the pair of dangling scalps. That's about when my pa and the other men rode out to see what was going on.

"Let's go down there, Jared," Kate said. "I'll bet our daddy's going to tell that Hogg a thing or two."

"You want to go down where those dead boys are? Their heads are all bloody."

She pressed her lips together. "Yes."

So we ran down there just as Pa and the others rode up.

"What in the hell is this, Hogg?" Pa asked.

"We done got us some Injun scalps, Mr. Sunnedon. Ain't they pretty?"

"This is an outrage. Those were two human beings."

"Red niggers is what they was," Hogg said. "Vermin."

"You sonofabitch. You'll bring the whole tribe down on us. That's no way for a civilized man to act."

Hogg just laughed. And so did Truitt. Kate and I got there breathless, and could see the anger on our father's face. The other men were pretty uneasy too.

"Don't you be calling me no damned names, Mr. Sunnedon. This is the goddamned West and civilization's rules don't count for dog shit."

"You ought to be whipped like a cur, Hogg," our pappy said. "A common cur."

"All right, Sunnedon, I've had about enough shit from you. You get your wagon out of my train. I don't want you in my camp tonight."

"Fine with me, Hogg. You damned butcher."

Our father turned to us, his face almost purple with rage.

"Jared, you and Kate get on back. We're packing up."

"Yes, sir," I said.

Kate whimpered and squeezed my hand.

But I stood there, rooted like a hickory to the spot, looking at those dead boys, with their heads all bloodied. Then, Hogg stuffed the scalp in his hand behind his belt.

"You folks go on back too," Hogg said. "Me 'n Truitt got some more surgery to perform here."

"What are you going to do?" Mr. Prentiss asked.

"You better not ask that question, Mr. Prentiss, unless you really got to know."

"I think you've done enough for one day, Mr. Hogg," Bandini said in that gravelly voice of his. "And I don't think you can just run Mr. Sunnedon off like that. He has a contract with you to take him to Oregon, same as us."

"Oh, didn't I tell you, Giacomo? I ain't takin' none of you to Oregon. We're heading for Santa Fe. I changed my mind about Oregon."

"You can't do that," Prentiss spluttered.

"I'm a-doin' it," Hogg said, then knelt back down and lifted the breechclout on one of the dead boys and cut away his privates as if he were slicking plums off a tree branch.

My stomach churned at the blood and I tightened my whole crotch up as if I was the one being castrated. Kate leaned over and lost her breakfast. It came spuming out like a jet of water, only it was a mess of johnnycakes and I don't know what all.

I grabbed her around the waist and pulled her toward our horses just as Truitt was putting the knife to the other boy's private parts. I heard Bandini get sick too, and when I looked at Prentiss, his face was white as bone.

That night, Pa was studying the stars, drawing up a route that would take us over the mountains to Oregon. He had a fix on the North Star, I knew. We were all alone on that vast prairie under a gleaming dark carpet of stars. I had never felt so lonesome in my life, nor more relieved in being away from Hogg and Truitt.

"Do you think we can make it, Pa?" I asked.

"Others have made it before us, Jared. We can do the same."

We were not so far from our wagon that we could not hear Ma and Kate crying softly. And after that, it was so quiet, it seemed like we were in a big old empty church with the night sky for a ceiling.

Two

The next morning I told Pa what I had heard after he left Hogg and Truitt to go back to our wagon and pack up.

"Hogg had no intention of leading us to Oregon, Pa."

"What?"

"That's what he told Mr. Bandini and Mr. Prentiss yesterday."

"That scurrilous bastard. You know, he wouldn't refund any of our money either."

"I know. Ma was pretty riled about that last night."

"I should have known," Pa said.

"About Oregon?"

"No, about Cassius Hogg. I heard stories about him back in Kansas City."

"What stories?"

Ma was driving the wagon, with Kate sitting beside her on the buckboard seat, so they couldn't hear what we were talking about. We rode ahead of the wagon on the two horses we had, a bay mare we called Sally, and a five-year-old gelding

Pa called Tuck, after Friar Tuck. Tuck was on the heavy side and would never win any races at the county fair.

"Oh, that he was a drunkard and a bully, a wastrel. But I never heard of him stranding anyone on the prairie before. Or taking people where they didn't want to go."

"Maybe Hogg said that to the others just to scare them."

"Maybe. I'm plumb burned that he didn't refund any of the money I gave him."

"That's stealing, Pa."

"Yeah. But he and Truitt were ready to jump me back there. I thought discretion was the better part of valor. If I ever see Hogg again, I'll make him pay what he owes me."

"How?"

"There are courts. Laws."

"Where we're going?"

Pa smiled. "I reckon," he said.

There were buttes and mesas rising from the broad land like ancient galleons, and in the distance, the Rocky Mountains. The sky was pure blue, and little puffs of white clouds floated here and there. Birds flew across our lines of sight every so often and we sometimes heard quail piping. Everything seemed so peaceful as we rode that unknown land. Small herds of buffalo grazed under the watchful eyes of a pronghorn sentinel standing near its flock, and best of all, the memory of Cassius Hogg was fading like the mist of morning on that soft, serene day.

The land turned gently rolling and we saw furrows lined with rocks and brush, devoid of trees. I looked atop every butte and majestic mesa, wondering if I would see an Indian scout, but there was only the sweep and sprawl of a land basking in the sun like some sleepy landscape a painter might put to canvas from a palette rich with burnt umber, cerulean, cobalt blue, white, brown, and black.

We stopped at noon, when the sun was straight up overhead, so Ma could make us lunch. She parked our wagon in the shadowy lee of a small bluff, so we had shade. She shooed off a rattlesnake before she laid out the tablecloth. You would have thought she was swatting at a pesky fly. But that was our mother. She wasn't afraid of anything. And when she could, she let critters be, saying they had as much right to life as we did. But we all knew that if any critter went to bite her, she would not shrink from exterminating it from the face of the earth. She had a kind of inner balance that I envied. Pa called it common sense. I called it uncommon sense.

Kate helped set out the foodstuffs, while Pa made himself scarce with his rifle, saying he might get us some fresh meat for supper. Kate and I tried to hide our snickers. Ma gave us dirty looks. I combed through my books and got out Homer's *Odyssey*, a book I never tired of reading. It seemed to me that we were on a journey like Odysseus, into a strange world where nothing was familiar. The prairie was our sea, and the gods were watching.

I leaned up against the rock wall of the bluff. The stone was cool on my back, a blessing in the heat of that day. I opened my book and started reading the poet Homer's words. They transported me away from that place and all others, into his world of peril and adventure. I lost track of time, and failed to hear the pounding of my father's footsteps as he ran back to the wagon from wherever he had been.

I heard Kate scream. And then Ma called out to me, and my pa yelled something I couldn't understand.

"Be quiet," Pa said to all of us. "We're not in any danger."

"But those are wild Indians," Ma said.

I got up, still holding Homer in my hand, and ran over to where my father and mother stood holding Kate between them.

"They're hideous," Ma said as the painted warriors rode up.

"That's war paint," Pa said. "But we're not at war with them. Whoever they are."

The Indians started yelling and brandishing their weapons, old Army rifles and lances. They surrounded us, and one of them stepped his pony up close to all of us and looked down at us. He spoke in a guttural, halting tongue, and made sign with his hands. He pointed to his head and made a circular motion with his index finger. He then held his empty arms up as if he were carrying a rifle and pulling the trigger with his right index finger.

"What's he saying?" Pa asked me.

"I think he's asking if we shot those two Indian boys and scalped them."

"No, no," Pa said, and shook his head.

Ma held Kate tight to her. I looked up and saw that her face was drawn, her eyes bright. But she was not afraid. Kate was afraid.

The leader spoke some words to the other braves. Some dismounted and held rifles on us, while three others went to our wagon. One crawled inside; another climbed up into the seat and bent over, searching for something with his fingers. The last crawled under the wagon on his back and looked underneath.

"What are they doing?" Ma asked.

"They're searching our wagon for something," Pa said.

"Well, they won't find anything," Ma said. She drew herself up tall and glared at the Indians surrounding us. She had a defiant look on her face, while my insides were squirming as if they were swarming with oily red worms. Kate shook as if she had the ague and her lips were quivering in fear.

There was a cry from inside the wagon. None of the Indians around us moved, but we prisoners looked over to the wagon. So did the leader, who still sat his pony, his face scrawled with paint, red, white, and black. His dark brown eyes flashed with what looked to me like both a warning and a look of satisfaction.

"Hunh," the leader grunted as the Indian in the wagon scrambled out, holding something in his hand. Something that danced as he ran over to the man on horseback. Something that shimmered and shimmied, flashed silver streaks on the dangling black hair of the scalps in his hand. Two scalps.

The Indian handed the scalps up to his leader and spat out some words that sounded as if they were hacked up from an afflicted throat. The leader grunted as he held up the two scalps and looked at them.

Ma gasped.

Pa swallowed. I could see his Adam's apple move up and down as if he had a chicken bone in his throat.

Then the Indian looked straight at Pa and said two English words.

"You kill."

Pa shook his head. So did I.

"Two boy," the leader said, and he held up two fingers. "Shoot dead."

"No, that was Cassius Hogg who did that." Pa pointed back in the direction we had come. "That bastard must have planted those scalps in our wagon."

I could see that the Indian didn't understand what Pa was trying to tell him. So I spoke up.

"The wagon boss shot those two Indian boys," I said. I made what sign I knew, swelling out my chest to imitate Hogg's size and bulk, holding an imaginary rifle and pulling an imaginary trigger. I made the sign of Hogg cutting my own scalp and pointed back to where Pa had pointed.

The leader spoke to the men in front of us. I didn't know what he said, but one of them laid his rifle down on the ground and drew a hatchet from his belt. Then he walked up to my father and struck him with the hatchet, splitting his head and face. My father's head spurted blood and he dropped like a sack of potatoes. My mother screamed and started to bend down to help my father. The Indian brought his hatchet down as she bent her head. The blade severed her spine and she stiffened. He hacked again, very hard, and separated her head from her body. It rolled away, Ma's mouth still working, but no sound coming out, her eyes glazing over with the frosty mist of death. Kate screamed a high-pitched sob of hysterical proportions that sent a shivering chill down my spine.

I heard my father gurgle and then his body went limp. There was a pool of blood around his head that soaked into the ground but left a crimson pool that quickly attracted flies.

The Indian with the hatchet stood up and looked me in the eyes without showing any visible emotion. I felt my stomach swirl with bile and knew I was going to be sick in a minute. The horror of the previous several seconds had me in its grip and I felt rooted to the ground, lifeless, while still barely breathing. Kate crumpled in a heap next to our mother. She was sobbing with uncontrollable grief, and I felt an invisible hand squeezing my heart. I dropped the book in my hand. It just fell out as my grip on it relaxed. It made a clattering sound as it landed on its spine and the pages rattled with a gust of breeze. The Indian on horseback, who seemed to be some kind of chief, looked down at it and his eyes glinted, even in the shadow of the towering bluff behind me.

The leader barked another guttural order to his braves, and three of them moved toward me. I stepped over to Kate and pulled her up, clasped her in my arms. I knew I couldn't protect her, but I didn't want her to die alone. She was still crying, and I felt her trembling body pressing against mine. I tightened my arms around her. The swirling sickness in my belly evaporated and turned to iron. I glared up at the leader.

Just before the painted warriors reached us, I took a deep breath and turned coward. I closed my eyes so that I would not see my death coming. I heard the whispers of their moccasins as they came for us. I waited in the darkness of my mind for certain, violent death.

Three

Rough hands grabbed me, and I felt Kate being snatched away from me.

I opened my eyes.

The Indians jerked us roughly over to the wagon. One of them carried the book I was reading with him, and he shoved it into my hands. I looked up at the leader, and he had a strange look on his face.

"You bring talking paper," he said in English. I heard a shuffling inside the wagon, and a brave emerged carrying my other books and an empty grain sack. He put the books inside the sack and handed it to me in a triumphant gesture. Two men held Kate's arms so that she could not run away, but none of them laid a hand on me after they gave me the sack of books.

I stood there as the braves swarmed over our parents with drawn knives and hatchets. They castrated my father and cut off his penis, the same way that Hogg had mutilated those two Indian boys. They took his scalp and the scalp of our mother. They cut away her private parts, but I couldn't look. I turned away when they cut away her drawers after hiking her dress up to her belly. It was a sickening sight, one that I will never forget.

The last thing the Indians did to my parents made me sick to my stomach and I doubled over and heaved my breakfast. Two of the Indians picked up clumps of grass and dirt and stuffed them into our parents' mouths, chanting some unintelligible gibberish as they did so. I came up for air and noticed that Kate's eyes were closed so tight, her eyelids were the color of pale alabaster. I started to say something to her, and just got her name out of my mouth when one of the braves backhanded me across the mouth so hard I tasted the salt in my blood.

I was nearly numb after that. The leader signed for us to get on our two horses, Kate and I. I had the bag of books with me, which, for some reason, the leader considered important. While we were mounted and waiting, the other Indians ransacked the wagon, stuffing food and other items into flour and gunnysacks. Some of the Indians peed on the bodies of our folks during all this pillaging. I heard the *plunk plunk plunk* of my mother's piano, and then something smashed into the keys, producing one last discordant chord. And then silence as the last of the thieving Indians emerged from the wagon and carried their ill-gotten loot to their ponies, which they mounted so expertly, I marveled at their litheness and agility.

The leader of the Indians made sign with his hands and we all followed him. There were Indians in front of Kate and me, and some behind and on both sides. We would not escape if these painted copper-skinned men had anything to say about it. Which, of course, they did.

We rode a long way toward the mountains, closer now,

but still a long way off. There was lots of buffalo sign, hoof marks, snubbed grass, and cow dung. Finally, we came to a stream that meandered across the prairie. There were cottonwoods growing along its course. We were so close I could smell the bark and the must of their leaves, and now could see unshod pony hoof marks in the soft dirt alongside the creek.

Much to my surprise, we did not go to the mountains that day. Instead, the land sloped beneath us and we came upon a small lake, perhaps ten acres in size, where a dozen teepees glistened white in the sun. Silver ripples gleamed in the waters of the lake. There was the smell of drying meat and fish wafting our way on the afternoon air.

A rider on the ridge above the camp raised his arm and waved a spear toward us. One of the Indians in our party shook his spear, and the people along the shore and in the teepees streamed toward us, men, women, children. They lifted a joyous shout when the leader of our small caravan held up the scalps of my parents. My stomach turned.

The name of the leader, I learned, was One Dog, Heth Casey in his native tongue. The Indians were of the Arapaho tribe. Kate and I were not beaten, but she was given to a family, while I was taken to One Dog's lodge, where I was stripped of my clothing and provided with only a breechclout made of deer hide and a pair of unbeaded moccasins. When next Kate made an appearance, that night by the fire when the warriors danced and bragged about their victory and our capture and told of the death of the two young boys, she was wearing a deerskin dress, also unbeaded, and moccasins similar to mine. The women keened and their tongues made trilling sounds over the reenactment of the murder of the two boys, while Kate and I were subjected to many hostile stares from the children and the women. The men seemed to ignore us. Kate looked frightened, and I knew she was, for she cringed between two girls about her own age and seemed to shrink back away from the dancing fire.

Kate was lodged with a family who treated her as a slave. She was made to do the washing and help with the cooking, hunt for firewood and buffalo chips. She was taught how to skin an antelope and do beadwork, make dresses out of elk skin and deerskin, moccasins, breechclouts, leggings, and such. The woman who ordered her about was called Biikosiis, or Moon Woman.

Yes, I was learning the spoken language of the Arapaho, who called themselves Inuna-Ina, which I learned meant merely "our people." But I soon realized why One Dog wanted me in his lodge and why he had made me bring my books. He wanted to learn how to decipher and write English words.

"Teach talking paper to One Dog," he told me the next morning. I soon learned that he spoke, besides some English, fairly fluent French, of which I had only a smattering, taught me by my mother, who told me that it was a dignified language, spoken all over the world.

I taught One Dog how to write, and later, to read. He was not dim-witted, but the symbols of the alphabet were difficult for him to grasp. When I realized this, I devised a way to relate the letters to him that formed the words.

I started with the word "tree." I drew a tree on my tablet, a crude tree at that. As he watched, I added leaves and fruit. He understood this. Then I drew a "T" and showed him how it related to the tree I had drawn. I made a small "r" and said that was like one of the branches on a tree. The two "e" letters, I showed him, were like the fruit. One Dog responded with glee when he was able to write the letters himself and say the word "tree." I showed him the "I" explaining that it represented a man, tall and straight.

We began to put simple sentences together, starting with "I am." I made the letter "A" as a capital letter and explained it as a teepee when it was standing as a lodge. Then I showed him the small letter "a," telling him that this was the teepee when it was balled up and ready to load on a travois. I explained to him what "I am" meant, and told him the "m" was a symbol of his shoulders. I made him see pictures in his mind, and he seemed never to tire of learning new letters and new words. And even I became fascinated with the process, finding new magic and mystery in the words, in language.

I taught him to write his name in English. I also showed him numerals and told him our counting system was based on the number 10. This was difficult. He did understand how to read and write the word "dog" very easily, however, when I told him the "d" was a dog sitting down with its paws held up. I demonstrated a sitting dog with my own body. The "o," I explained, was how the dog looked when it was lying down with only its butt showing. And the "g" was its curly tail. With the word "one" I had to be more creative, and told him the "o" was the circle of life, which he had explained to me one day when he first saw the "o." The "n" was a horse's track, signifying that the circle was connected to the horse. And the "e" was the "fruit" the horse left behind, what we called "horse apples," and which One Dog understood perfectly. Teaching him to read and write was not difficult, but just thinking up ways to come up with symbols that he could relate to was taxing, and I was worn out every night just from the effort of using hand signs and coming up with solutions One Dog could understand. In this way, however, I began to learn his language while he was learning mine.

But all the time I was teaching One Dog, I was planning on my escape, knowing how difficult it would be for me and Kate to escape the watchful eyes of the tribe. I learned too that one of the boys who had been killed was One Dog's only son, and he told me his wife had been killed by Utes, somewhere up in the Medicine Bow Mountains, which he told me were far away from where we now were. He drew me a crude map in the dirt, to show me where the mountain range lay from our camp by the small lake.

Other Arapaho bands joined us, and the teepees along the shore became more numerous. One Dog said they would all soon leave to hunt buffalo, but the added numbers gave me the chance to plan my escape. I began to steal small items that I would need to survive. I realized that if they were all kept in one place, there was a likelihood that one of the Arapaho would discover my cache. So I selected several hiding places, scattered all over, under rocks, buried carefully in the ground, in places where children, women, and braves seldom walked. I left a chunk of flint in one place, striking steel in another. I filched rifle balls and powder, small amounts that I hid in various places.

I saw little of Kate, who was kept busy, but one day we had a chance to talk for a few minutes when Moon Woman came by to see One Dog. As the two Arapaho were talking together, I whispered to Kate.

"We're going to escape, Kate, you and me. Just give me time."

"They will kill us if we try and do that."

"A day will come when our chances are good. Can you make extra clothes for us that I can hide somewhere?"

She shook her head. "I don't know. I don't think so."

"Try, will you?"

"I'll try," she said, and then we had to stop talking.

The Arapaho made preparations for the buffalo hunt and I learned that afterward, they would all journey to a place where they would hold their annual Sun Dance, a sacred ceremony that I knew nothing about.

One morning, the camp emptied of men as they all rode off to the hunt. The women and children began to strike the teepees. They loaded all their belongings onto travois, using poles they had cut from wood I never saw long before Kate and I had been captured. We left the lake and followed the pony tracks.

All of the things I had stolen and hidden had to be left behind, but I knew I could find the place again when the time came for me to grab Kate and make my escape. I would have to keep my wits about me and remember every stretch of that journey to the buffalo hunt, not an easy task in such vastness as I saw along the way.

Kate didn't give me any clothing, but she gave me what she could, sinew, needles, and scraps of tanned hide that could be sewn together for wearing apparel. She did this the night before we left the lake, and I hid everything in new places that I hoped I would remember, digging in the ground until my fingernails were clogged with dirt.

When the time came to make my escape, I knew I would have to kill One Dog and perhaps some others. I would have to steal two horses for Kate and me and make my way back to the lake.

And I knew I had to do this before the Arapaho journeyed to the place where they would hold their Sun Dance.

Time was now my enemy.

Four

We journeyed across the prairie for most of the night. I felt like an outcast, because I was the oldest male member of that caravan and the women and children all watched me as if they were circling hawks. It was a humiliating experience and the fact that I was a prisoner, among people who had murdered our parents, made the experience even more intolerable.

The motley caravan halted sometime well after midnight. We were all dog-tired, sleepy, and hungry. Most of the people just dropped to the ground next to the travois. Some of the women laid out blankets, buffalo robes, and such, while others fed the horses, leaving the travois hooked up. But the young boys propped forked sticks under the poles to take some of the weight off the horses' shoulders.

I knew we would not rest long. It was pitch-dark at that hour, but I reckoned that when the sky began to pale and the stars fade, the women of the tribe would have us up and moving again. I was just starting to drop off into a deep sleep when a hand touched my face and I heard a whispered voice calling my name.

"Jared, Jared. Are you asleep?"

It was Kate. Her shape was just an inky shadow above my face, but it was her voice all right, and the words were in plain, everyday English.

"Yeah. Kate?"

"I snuck off. Do you want to run away now? While everybody's asleep?"

"We wouldn't get very far. All the horses are hooked up to travvy poles."

"I know," she whispered. "But we could steal just one and ride double."

I looked around. The camp, such as it was, was quiet, except for the snuffle of a feeding horse and the snores of the old women. The stars were bright, and so was the silver moon riding high above us like a round sailing ship. We would have to move very fast and hope that none of the young boys left behind could catch us, or shoot us in the back with arrows. The boys all had bows and full quivers.

"I hate it here, Jared," she said, her voice almost a whimper. "We've got to get away."

"Yes, I know. First, we'll have to find a horse we can take."

"At the other end of the camp," she said, "there's a little boy sleeping under the travois. He's all by himself. Do you know how to take the poles off?"

"Yes. I think so."

"Then let's go," she said.

I got up and followed Kate around the edge of the sleeping camp. We both hunched over as if we were sneaking away on tiptoes. We were careful not to make any noise, but it was so quiet, except for the snoring, and the snuffling of the horses. Kate stopped and pointed. There, at the far edge of the encampment, was a lone horse and a lightly loaded travois. I nodded and took the lead.

I crept up on the horse and the boy sleeping under the high side of the travois. He wasn't a small boy, as I had thought, but a big, nearly full-grown boy, who might have been as old as I was. He was sound asleep, so I crept past him and motioned for Kate to go on the other side and lift the poles out of their loops. My idea was to drop the travois on top of the boy, climb up on the horse, and pull Kate up behind me. The horse was wearing a halter, but not a bridle. I knew the Indians used their knees to guide their ponies, and some even pulled on their ponies' manes to turn them. The halter was woven out of horsehair, I think, but looked substantial enough so that I would have some control over the animal.

Kate snuck around the other side and looked at me. I held up three fingers, then closed my fist. I was hoping she'd know what I meant, that we would release the poles on the count of three. She nodded and I held up my hand, then extended one finger, then another, then the last. We both lifted the poles and pushed backward.

As soon as the poles came free, the pony spooked. I lunged for the halter, but it was too late. The pony bolted and kicked at me. His hoof struck me just above the knee, a glancing blow. But the pain was intense and I went down on one knee. Kate shrieked, cut the sound off, but not before she woke up half the camp. The travois fell on the boy, who rolled out from under it and grabbed me around the neck as I tried to rise up and stand on both feet. The pony ran through the camp, scared out of its wits apparently, and people rose up and shouted.

Kate came over and started beating the boy who had ring-necked me, pounding his back with her small fists. I turned and squirmed out of the boy's grip, but he grabbed my arm and held on like a bulldog. Kate kicked him, and he swatted her with a backhanded swing of his left arm. She went staggering off into the darkness as I tried to loosen the boy's grip on my arm.

With high-pitched screeches and screams, Indian women and children swarmed over Kate as I fought with the boy, pushing and shoving him, trying to strike blows to his face with my fists. Some other boys ran up and piled onto me. I went down under a mass of bodies, then felt sharp pains as some of the boys kicked me in my sides.

In moments, it was all over. Two boys jerked me to my feet. Everyone around me was jabbering in rapid Arapaho. A boy came up in front of me carrying a smooth slender pole that resembled a straight walking stick. Two other boys forced my arms over my head and the boy with the stick laid it across my shoulders. Then the other two boys tied my arms to the stick with leather thongs, pulling them so tight they cut into my flesh.

Some of the women and young girls poked my chest with sharp, pointed sticks, drawing blood. I was kicked and drubbed as they led me away to the front of the camp, where a boy hurled me to the ground and cursed me in his native tongue. Kate was nowhere to be seen, but I suspected she had suffered a similar fate.

A ring of boys squatted down, surrounding me. Some jabbed me with the flint tips of their arrows, again drawing blood. The stick made my shoulders and arms hurt. All during this ordeal, I never gave them the satisfaction of crying out, although the beatings made my whole body hurt and I was sure that I was covered with bruises. The boys who were guarding me taunted me, called me every kind of filthy name. I was dog shit and snake shit. I was skunk and lizard. I was bad white boy and I was bad milk from my father's testicles. I knew some of the cuss words, but I kept my mouth shut.

Finally, the kickers left me alone. I lay there, trussed up like a Christmas turkey, the wood shaft digging into my shoulder blades, ants crawling all over my arms and legs and face, trying to hold my piss. My bladder was full and had been kicked something fierce, so it was ready to explode. The sky started to pale and the camp began to stir. I had no idea what they had done to Kate or where they had taken her, but I was hoping she wasn't in pain, like I was.

Some boys jerked me roughly to my feet. I pissed on one boy's leg, and he smacked me across the mouth. I grinned at him and he struck me again. I lunged for him and he backed away, saying something in Arapaho that I could understand.

"White boy brave," he said, and that gave me some satisfaction.

No one struck any fires and the band began to move. I saw the horse we had tried to steal, pulling its light travois, and the boy who was leading him saw me, lifted his breechclout, and displayed his pathetic genitals. All I could do was stick my tongue out at him, which I did. Little kids ran up behind me and stung my legs with switches, then ran away before I could kick them. They laughed at such sport with the white boy, and then finally left me alone when one of the women began scolding them.

The sun rose and bore down on me. I thought I knew a little about how Christ felt carrying that cross up to Calvary, but of course I had a lighter load. Still, I felt like I had been crucified, and I was damned mad at the entire tribe of

Arapaho. Near noon, those at the head of the procession halted and began directing the rest of us to form a circle. With relief, I realized that they were going to lay out a camp and set up the teepees. I didn't know how the women knew where to set up camp until I looked around and saw all the hollows where men had slept on the ground. And the place was crisscrossed with moccasin tracks.

Then, I felt the ground shake beneath my feet and I heard a rumbling sound. I thought at first that we were experiencing an earthquake, and then I saw the buffalo stream by in the distance. The others stopped what they were doing to look too. There were thousands of brown bodies running at high speed across the prairie. And I could make out near-naked Arapaho riding alongside, shooting arrows into the sides of certain buffalo. I saw the shaggy beasts go down, and the women lifted up their trilling cries and went back to work. Soon, the women were running from camp, carrying knives and bowls with them, while others struck fires from flint and stone. The bigger children ran off too, and I was left standing there with that yoke on my back like some dumb beast of burden.

Two boys guarded me, clearly angry that they could not join the others who were butchering the downed buffalo. I looked at one of them and nodded toward a teepee, hoping he would take me inside, out of the sun. But he only glared at me and moved off belligerently to stand in the shade of that same teepee.

Finally, late in the afternoon, the braves started streaming back into camp. One Dog rode up to me and looked down into my eyes.

"Bad heart," he said in English. "You bad. No run."

I shook my head, thinking that he wanted me to promise I would not try to run away again.

One Dog said something to the two boys who had been guarding me, and they ran off to join those who were butchering buffalo. Soon, some started walking back carrying meat and hides. Some of the women carried bowls that were filled with hearts and livers and buffalo intestines. The smells were terrible, but my stomach rumbled with hunger.

One Dog slid from his pony and untied the thongs that held the stick in place across my shoulders. He grabbed the stick before it fell to the ground, and then laid it across the backs of my legs with such force that I crumpled to my knees.

"You no run," he said, as if for emphasis.

Tears stung my eyes.

"One Dog is wise," I said in Arapaho. "One Dog is brave."

He actually smiled at me.

Then he beat me so hard my bones cracked and ached.

And I soaked the ground with my tears before he quit.

Five

After that, life was hell for me.

One Dog beat me whenever he was in camp, treated me like a dog. He still wanted me to teach him to read and write and he asked me questions about the books I read. I started making up stories from those books, making them sound as if they were legends of the Arapaho people.

There was much meat in camp and the people were happy. The women tanned the buffalo hides, made garments, blankets, and robes from them. They used every part of the buffalo, the bones, the sinew, the hides. They boiled the intestines and ate these. They were an industrious people and seemed very happy as the summer wore on.

I saw Kate now and then. She smiled at me to show me that she was all right.

One Dog finally stopped beating me, but he still tied me up at night. His English was improving and so was my knowledge of the Arapaho language, which seemed to have a basis of about eight or nine hundred words. They could pack a lot of meaning into those few words, I discovered, and once I understood how to think in Arapaho, I became fluent in the language.

But I didn't tell One Dog, nor anyone else, that I could understand every word of their language. I only used simple words, not sentences, when I spoke to him, or any other member of the tribe. I used words like "eat" and "hungry" to convey my meaning. When the people spoke to one another, I played dumb. I never let on that I could understand every blessed word they spoke.

I told One Dog the story of Odysseus, using sign and drawing pictures for him in the dirt of our teepee. I told him that Odysseus was a great warrior and that all great warriors embarked on such journeys, including himself. I could see One Dog swell up with pride when I made the connection between him and Odysseus. I told him there were many such stories and that they were all written in a magic language that was neither English nor Arapaho. One Dog thought that the talking papers were magic, and he was eager to learn all their secrets. I played One Dog like a musician strokes the strings of a fiddle, and I bided my time.

When the buffalo herd had gone away and the camp was full of meat and work for the women and children and men, there was talk of the great Sun Dance at a faraway river. Soon, the new bands that had joined the camp began making preparations to embark on still another journey toward the place of the Sun Dance, a most sacred ceremony for the Arapaho.

The large band that had gathered to hunt buffalo thus began to split up. Each morning, one of the clans would

leave, until finally, there were left only our original number of twelve lodges. Then, finally, our camp struck its
teepees and loaded the travois. We left one morning, heading westward into lands where neither I nor Kate had
ever been.

The country seemed to spread out, then collapse into itself. The earth looked ravaged by ancient floods that cut
deep gullies and ravines into its surface. Buttes and mesas
became more frequent, and larger, as if some great force
had pushed the earth up, packed it down, and turned it to
stone. The mountains grew ever closer, their snowcapped
peaks shining white in the sun, their dark hulks looming
over that vast plain like some fortress built by giants, or
gods. Sometimes, when I looked at them, my heart squeezed
up into my throat and I was dumbstruck.

At night, the stars seemed so close that I felt I could
reach up and touch them, and they twinkled like diamonds
on a sea of velvet, while the moon sailed so close it seemed
I could feel its beating heart. And when the moon fell close
to the horizon, it became a huge, luminous globe, so bright
it hurt my eyes to look at it.

Maybe that wasn't the Oregon Trail we were on, or
maybe it was and I just didn't know it. But I missed my father on those long star-shining nights, and my mother too.
We should all have been together, heading west, Ma, Pa,
Kate, and I, but Fate, that cruel, manipulative bastard, had
decreed differently.

As for Kate, my heart ached for her because I had noticed that she was no longer with Moon Woman, but was
living in the lodge of one of the men who had murdered our
parents. I found out that his name was Hiisiis Ba'a', Red
Sun. That's not exactly what his name meant, but that was
the literal translation. I learned, from listening to the talk in

One Dog's lodge, that Hiisiis Ba'a' really meant something like "His body is red with blood," and I shuddered at the expanded meaning of the Arapaho words.

I caught glimpses of Kate and she looked wan and tired, and sometimes I thought I could hear her animal cries in the night when Red Sun was mounting her. But my imagination ran rampant on that long trek and all of my thoughts about Kate and the Arapaho were probably suspect. I hated those red-skinned bastards with such a purity and silent rage that I was startled at how deep that hatred went and how fierce it burned in my heart, like the fire in our stove back home in Kansas City.

One morning, after the scouts had been sent out ahead and we were packing up to leave our overnight camp, one of the scouts rode back in at a high gallop. He was spewing words and signing with his hands so fast I couldn't follow him. But a moment later, I saw what he was so excited about. And smelled it.

The prairie was on fire. Flames danced like dervishes on the horizon and billows of smoke rose to the blue sky. The wind was in our faces as we looked westward, and it was evident that the fire was coming our way at a high rate of speed. One Dog barked orders to leave. The whole camp mobilized in jig time, and turned their backs to the fire and headed east. The boys lashed the rumps of the travois ponies with willow branches. Then One Dog held up his hand and everyone came to a halt. There was fire to the east of us, and more smoke.

The band turned northward, and we ran into still another wall of flame and more smoke. Back we turned to head south, and that's when we knew we were ringed in by a vast fire that covered many acres. Then the smoke blew in on us and we all began to choke and cough.

One Dog ordered his braves to dismount. The young boys hobbled the travois ponies and we all lay flat on the ground, breathing the only clean air that was available. There was smoke everywhere.

I noticed that the warriors ringed the villagers and all were armed. I wondered if they were going to shoot at the fire in a primitive attempt to stop it. Everyone grew very quiet and I felt fear tighten my belly, then rise up in my throat. I looked around at the faces of the others lying nearby, but they all seemed calm, fearless.

Then, my face close to the ground, I heard a faint rumbling. The noise grew louder and I wondered what it was. I lifted my head and looked at the naked backs of two braves who were facing south. They lifted their bows and knocked arrows to the gut strings.

I soon realized what the sound was. Hoofbeats.

The rumbling grew louder, and then I heard the high-pitched yips coming from somewhere inside the smoke. Suddenly, there appeared a pony out of the smoke and the rider was hunched over its back, his face painted for war.

Then more painted warriors dashed out of the smoke and the screeches tore at my ears, blasted my eardrums. Rifles spouted orange flames and I heard a lead ball whistle over my head. The Arapaho braves leaped to their feet and began shooting arrows and firing their rifles at the invaders who swept onto the gathering like hordes of locusts. There was pandemonium and confusion everywhere I looked. Women screamed. Children cried out in pain and fear. Men grunted, and some of them went down with arrows in their chests or their heads split open by rifle balls.

The Arapaho people were shouting *"Ota,"* and other words I didn't know at the time. At one time I heard the word *"Uintah"* as well, but it made no sense to me. I had never heard any of these words spoken before. But I knew that we were being attacked by a tribe of Indians who were not Arapaho. They looked different, with round moonlike faces and stocky bodies, and the beadwork on their loin-cloths and moccasins was different. So too, the paint patterns on their faces.

I looked around for a weapon so that I could defend myself or at least help ward off the savage attack. I found a lance and picked it up. That lance was like a magnet. The minute I had it in my hands, one of the marauders turned his pony and charged straight at me. He held a war club above his head and I knew he meant to brain me.

My scalp tingled when I saw him close the gap between us. I almost didn't have time to think. When he came within a few yards of me, I drew back my arm and hurled the lance with all my might. I was surprised that the weapon ran true, striking the warrior in the stomach, just below his ribs. The force of the lance pushed him backward. Blood gushed from his body. I dodged his pony as it ran by, dropping the warrior at my feet. There was a surprised look in his eyes. I stood there, frozen, as he squirmed. Blood bubbled up out of his mouth and his eyes glazed over and then closed.

I began to tremble all over. The trembles turned into violent shakes. I had killed a man. With my own hands, I had taken a human life. I lifted my head and gulped in air. The din around me began to diminish as the smoke got thicker. Then I heard hoofbeats as the invaders galloped off. Some were carrying women under their arms, and I saw a child wriggling as he lay across a pony's back, a warrior pinning him down in front of him.

Then it was quiet for just a second.

I breathed in air to try and get over the shakes.

That's when the Arapaho women began trilling with their tongues. There arose the sound of a terrible keening as people stumbled around, checking to see who had been kidnapped by the attacking Indians.

One Dog emerged out of the smoke and made a sign for us to follow him. I learned that most of the horses had been run off, stolen, and that two young women had been kidnapped, along with a small boy. Those were the ones the Arapaho counted. But there was one other person missing, and my heart sank like a stone in water when I learned of it.

The attacking Indians had also taken my sister, Kate.

We ran through the smoke, over burned and burning ground, until we were well away from the flames.

All of the travois, the teepees, the clothing, weapons, food, and utensils had been burned up. We were afoot. Even those horses that had belonged to my parents had been taken. The tribe had four ponies left, and that was about all.

That night we slept on bare ground in the open. I cried myself to sleep.

Kate was gone and I feared the worst. I sobbed and sobbed, wondering if I'd ever see her again.

Six

Not everything is burned in a fire. Any fire. After the flames burned out and left the land charred, the women and children went back to the place where we had been attacked and sifted through the ashes. They retrieved flint and steel, flint arrowheads, some clay utensils, some skin water bags, knives, and other tools and implements. Unknown to me, the Arapaho had already begun to track the marauders, who I learned were members of the Ute tribe.

We all followed the tracks after that, and I began to pay close attention to each pony's hoof marks and the shod tracks of my father's horses. I watched the Arapaho trackers, listened to them talk, and learned a great deal. One Dog left me to myself, as if he no longer cared, and perhaps that was because all of my books had burned in the fire. I found a few charred pages, but none were whole, and there was nothing to do but leave them on the burnt prairie and put them out of my mind.

It was sad to see what the prairie fire had done to the camp, and I began to feel sorry for the Arapaho who held me prisoner. The looks on the women's faces as they picked through the rubble became indelible in my mind. Although they did not weep or pull their hair, their eyes showed their sorrow, not only for the loss of their belongings, but for the loss of their children. I learned that the Arapaho looked upon children as belonging to the entire tribe, not to just one family.

One Dog's attitude toward me seemed to change after the attack. He told me he was sorry that the talking papers had been burned up, but said he hoped that I would tell him what was in the books and continue to teach him to read and write.

"I will have to write on dirt," I told him in sign language. "You will have to write on dirt."

"That was always the way with my people," he said, using both sign and speech.

I wondered if he knew that I could understand his language almost perfectly. If so, he said nothing about it, but I noticed that he began to talk more to me as we walked along, following the trail of the Utes.

He told me that a man could always walk down a horse and he said we would find the Utes and punish them, get back his ponies.

"The Ute," he said, "have ears of stone. They sneak like the snake and their hearts are as cold as the winter moon. They do not have good eyes, but are like the moles that live under the ground. They are blind."

"They found us," I said.

"As the mole finds the grasshopper. We did not see them coming. We did not hear them. We were like moles. But we

THE SUNDOWN MAN   39

have eyes now. We will find them and tear their hearts out and feed them to the wolf."

We did not find the Utes that day, nor the next. But from the freshness of the tracks, we were getting closer. On the third day of tracking, we did find something, something that still makes my blood run to ice.

The young Arapaho boy was lying on a rock, his arms and legs splayed until he resembled a disemboweled X. He had been gutted and scalped, his private parts cut away, his heart snatched from the center of his open chest. He was a ghastly sight, and I vomited for five minutes while the women screamed and trilled their death songs.

One Dog's face was an inscrutable mask, but his dark eyes glinted like moonstruck agates, flashing a hatred that was almost palpable.

The boy's body was still warm, whether from the sun or his recent death was uncertain. But I touched his neck, and it was still supple and bore heat, although his head was cocked so that this part of him was in the shade. His eyes had been plucked out too, and I nearly vomited again when I saw the empty sockets.

We were traveling south, very near the mountains now, and the Ute tracks got fresher with every moment that passed.

"They make the horses run," One Dog said. "The Ota will kill the horses."

There were Arapaho scouts ahead of us, out of sight, running, walking, running again, to close the distance. I hoped the Utes, or Ota, as the Arapaho called them, would not kill Kate like they had killed that poor Arapaho boy.

I began to fully realize what had been festering inside me for some time, even when we were back in Kansas City, before my family ever dreamed of going west. The world wasn't what I was brought up to believe, a benevolent place where neighbors were kind to neighbors and violence was something that happened far away and always to someone else. Even back there, in civilization, I had an inkling that what I had been taught in Sunday school, to follow the Ten Commandments, to obey the law and mind my parents, was only a set of rules and guidelines that very few humans followed.

When I was about seven or eight, the man across the street, who had always seemed quiet and kindly toward all of us, murdered his entire family one night. He hacked his wife to death with an ax while she was asleep, and then stabbed his two little daughters and his son, and for good measure, slit their throats. People said he was crazy, and that accounted for the atrocity as far as they were concerned. But I later found out that the man was a philanderer. He had a mistress and she didn't want his children, only him. So, he killed his family. They were obstacles in his path.

Later, as I grew up, I began reading the newspapers my father brought home. In their pages they listed all sorts of crimes, and many of these involved murders, usually among family members. When I asked my parents about these things, they called them aberrations of society, and said that most people were honest, hardworking, and law-abiding. But I began to form a picture in my mind that this was not entirely true.

Some men held up the bank in our town and they murdered innocent people. Eyewitnesses, as reported in the newspaper, said there was no need for the robbers to kill anyone. A little boy murdered his playmate. I went to school with both boys. The killer said he wanted a toy the other boy had and when he wouldn't give it to him, he picked up a rock and smashed the kid's head so hard it split open, and the murdered boy bled to death.

In the short time I had spent out West, I learned that not only did animals hunt other animals for food, but everything seemed to feed on everything else, and tribes of Indians not only killed whites, but fought among themselves, killing, not for food, but for horses, trinkets, goods, and trophies such as scalps.

Now, after seeing that splayed bloody boy on the rock, I measured my world in a different way. All people were born killers. Some killed out of necessity, self-defense, while others killed for greed or other kinds of gain. Some just killed out of pure hatred, and I had seen those kinds of murders in the newspapers too. At the taverns, there were always fights and some men died by knife or gun.

And now, I had killed a man myself.

I wondered if my motive was survival, or had I killed out of anger, rage?

It was a question that would puzzle me for some time, but there was blood on my hands now and it was something I knew I had to deal with if I was ever to come to terms with it. Deep in the pit of my being, I knew I was going to kill again. I just didn't know when.

There were signs that the Ota ponies were tiring. The hoof marks showed signs of dragging, an indication of weariness. The two shod horses seemed to be faring better. They were larger, they were shod, and they weren't being ridden apparently.

One of the scouts rode in, late in the afternoon. His spotted pony bore streaks of sweat, showing that he had ridden fast during some part of his quest. I moved close to One Dog to hear what the Arapaho warrior had to say. He didn't use words, but forked the finger of one hand with the other, indicating a rider on horseback. He moved his hands to show the direction. Then he pointed to the mountains.

So, the Ota had changed course. They were now heading for the mountains. Perhaps there, they planned an ambush or would find better means of concealment. One Dog grew excited, and he spoke to those braves still with us, and to the women and children. He too used sign language, and we immediately started angling toward the mountains.

Then another scout rode in, leading the horse of another. And draped over the back of the other horse was an Arapaho brave, dead or unconscious. People rushed to take the body from the horse while the rider who had led it in spoke to One Dog telling him what had happened.

The Ota, or Utes, as I had learned they were called, had doubled back and attacked the scouts in flanking movements. They had come close and smashed the limp brave with a war club. The brave's name was Walking Wolf. He was still alive, but there was a bloody clot behind his ear, covering a deep gash. They laid him out and people stood over him to give him shade. The women washed the wound and applied some leaves and mud to the wound. Some of the women chanted, praying to the Great Spirit to spare the life of Walking Wolf.

But an hour later, the young man died. He went into convulsions and no amount of chanting could bring him back.

We continued our pursuit of the Ota, all the while edging toward the mountains. I could feel them loom closer. The foothills stood out in stark relief as the day wore down and the sun hung above the snowcapped peaks. A wind came up, and it seemed to come from those high peaks. It was fresh and cool. The shadows of the foothills stretched out toward us. We were no longer following tracks. The

Arapaho seemed to know where the Ota were going. So I figured that this was familiar territory to both tribes.

I worried about Kate, and the knot in my stomach tightened. I thought about my dead parents and their dream of going to Oregon. Where, they said, the grass would be greener.

I was not so sure that there existed any such place.

What I was finding out was that the grass was not greener on the other side.

The grass was bloodier.

Seven

The Arapaho carried the body of Walking Wolf into the foothills. Scouts came back with cut poles and they built a scaffold before sunset. They placed the dead warrior's body atop the scaffolding, prayed and chanted quietly, then moved on, deeper into the hills. We spent the night on top of a ridge, with scouts riding in and out of camp all night. I knew they were looking for the Ota, but the thought gave me no peace. Kate was out there somewhere too, perhaps being ravaged by moonfaced young men who had never plumbed a white girl before. The thought twisted me inside so tight I could not eat nor sleep.

To my surprise, after all that had happened, One Dog still wanted to learn the English language. More than that, he showed a keen interest not only in Greek mythology, but in plumbing the depths of the white man's mind. He asked a great many questions while the braves were tracking the Ota, and at night, when we ate fresh-killed game, deer, partridge, quail, rabbit, and antelope.

"You have many spirit beings," he said during one of our talks. "Those who are called gods."

"No. The white man has only one god. The Greeks, and the Romans, had many."

"The people have many such gods too," he told me.

"But only one who is chief."

"Yes, that is true."

"It is the same with the Greeks. One chief, many gods. They have a god of wind, of the big water, hunting, and growing food to eat."

"That is good," he said. "It is good to have many gods. Many spirits, but only one Great Spirit."

"So, the people are like the Greek people."

"You have much wisdom for your few years."

He knew my name, could pronounce it, but when he asked me its meaning, I could not give him an answer. One Dog thought that very strange.

He decided that I must have an Arapaho name, but I was against it. I did not want to become an Arapaho, and I suspected One Dog harbored fatherly feelings toward me. When I told him I did not want a name by which his people would call me, he said only that he would call me "White Man," Hinen Namaacaa', and I accepted that as descriptive rather than nominal. But of course, I did not tell One Dog my feelings. I still harbored a deep hatred of him and his people, although something inside me was beginning to change as we hunted the even more terrible Ota, who had kidnapped my sister, Kate.

Much as I resisted being named by a savage, that very act by One Dog affected a profound change in me, despite my resistance to any change in my thinking concerning the Arapaho people. Or perhaps it was the language that began the subtle movement toward change in my mind.

Language, I realized, was a key to understanding foreign people. In order to understand the Arapaho, I had to think as they did, no matter how difficult that might be. And in thinking like them, I wondered if I was not becoming like them.

The Arapaho became human.

I realized that when I lay down that night after One Dog had given me an Arapaho appellation, if not an outright name. In seeing these people as human beings like myself, it seemed I was no longer a prisoner, no longer living with an enemy. I thought of the women of the tribe, how the mothers sat quietly as their daughters combed their long hair, and when a mother would comb her daughter's hair, I saw my own mother running a comb through Kate's tresses at night, and Kate gently and tenderly combing my mother's hair, tirelessly stroking the strands with the teeth of the comb until my mother's hair was sleek and shiny, glowing in the amber lamplight like spun gold.

The women and girls of the Arapaho tribe suddenly had faces and eyes I could look into and see that they loved one another and cared for each other, just as Kate and Mother had loved and cared for each other. I did not see tender signs of affection from men toward the women, their wives and daughters, but I saw the light in the women's eyes when they looked at their husbands, their fathers. They were like the secret looks I saw in my mother's eyes when she looked at my father, and like the light in Kate's eyes when our father patted her hair or gave her a compliment.

I lay there, wrestling with such thoughts, unable to sleep, wondering about myself, the changes in me that had crept into my being without my knowing, unbidden, unforeseen. These people, the Arapaho, were my enemies. They had murdered my parents, stolen us, and had set in motion the events that took Kate away from me. I was an orphan and felt sorry for myself, and I was ashamed that I thought this, felt this.

I began to wonder about One Dog, what kind of life he had lived. Were his parents dead, perhaps killed by white men or Indians from another tribe? Was he too an orphan? I could not yet fathom any of the relationships between the men and women of the tribe. I could observe the women, the girls and boys, but I did not know their feelings for one another. They did not seem expressive toward one another, yet I could feel those strong bonds between parents and children. Indeed, the children belonged to each older member of the tribe, and that was a puzzle to me. That was an expression of love, of deep love, yet it remained almost unfathomable to my young mind at that time.

I was even beginning to put names to some of the faces of my captors, making them seem even more human to me. It was easy to look at strangers and dismiss them as not worth my attention. What was difficult was finding the humanity in the lowliest of God's creatures. And when the Arapaho took me, I considered them nothing more than savage animals, without feelings, without morals, and without conscience. On that long thoughtful night, however, I began to look at the Arapaho much differently.

And that worried me.

The next morning, two of the scouts came riding in with news of the Ota. From their sign language, I figured out that they had come upon one of the ponies and thought the Ota must be near. There was much gesticulating and a lot of grunts and terse words from the scouts. One Dog listened with impassivity, and I thought I could see his mind working, although he merely grunted in assent every so often and made no comment about the discovery.

But the camp packed up to leave that place and go where the pony was supposedly waiting for all of us to see it. Scouts came and went, but it did not take long to find the pony. I recognized it as one of those belonging to the Utes, because it had markings painted on it that I had seen the day they attacked us. On its right shoulder was a round circle with a black spot in the center, and on the left shoulder a red feathered arrow. There was a lot excited conversation among those in the tribe who also recognized the pony.

One Dog was speaking to his braves and using sign language to augment what he was saying. All the time, he was looking around him, up through the hills, at ridges and ravines. He made a sign that was unmistakable since I had some experience back home in Missouri setting traps on a creek. One Dog held both hands together flat and opened and closed them.

He thought that the pony was a trap, and waved everyone to cover, ordered scouts to ride off in different directions.

At the same time, One Dog hefted his rifle and checked the pan of the flintlock to see if his powder was still there and still dry. The people began to run toward hiding places while One Dog and some of the braves covered them, peering into the bushes and the gullies for any sign of Ota.

A quail piped from somewhere up in the hills. One Dog stiffened, and the other braves swung their bows and rifles toward the sound. Another quail whistled from another place, lower down, closer. The braves dropped to their knees. A boy grabbed my arm and dragged me into a shallow depression below some rocks. The women and children all hunkered down and huddled like wet birds. There arose an awful silence.

Then the silence broke with a piercing, high-pitched screech. Utes poured from hiding places like angry hornets, swooping down toward One Dog and his men on galloping ponies that seemed to have appeared out of nowhere. More yelling and the crackle of rifle fire removed all doubt that we were surrounded and the Utes were riding in for the kill.

The Utes swooped down on top of us, some swinging war clubs, others shooting arrows at us. One had a Henry or a Winchester and was firing rapidly. He was afoot and try-ing to take careful aim. I saw him behind a bush, kneeling down on one leg, the rifle bucking against his shoulder with each shot. I had seen such a rifle before, in Hogg's pos-session. He said it was a new Winchester '73, and he had twenty of them that he hoped to sell out West when we got to Oregon. I wondered if he'd sold at least one to the Utes, or had bartered for his life with it. Anger boiled up in me when I thought about Cassius Hogg and his treachery.

The Arapaho put up a good fight, the braves running from place to place, avoiding bullets and arrows, dropping Utes from horses with their arrows and bullets from their guns. But some Arapaho men fell, bleeding, and another's head was split in two when a Ute brained him with a war club.

Some of the bigger boys ran out, picked up weapons from the fallen braves, and chased the Utes on foot, firing arrows at them, arrows that had no force nor direction.

Then, suddenly, the fight was over.

The Utes rode right on past us and headed south at a full gallop, voicing their victory cries. The women scrambled from their hiding places and fell upon the wounded men as if trying to breathe life into them. They dabbed at their bloody wounds with cloths and thin pieces of leather.

Some of the braves gave chase on horseback, but One Dog called the rest back. He had lost three good men and four others were badly wounded. Two boys were slightly hurt. Our small band was dwindling in number and the number of Ota scalps were but two, which a brave brought back to where we were, the locks dripping blood.

The women keened for the dead. The boys built burial scaffolds and One Dog organized the band, giving orders quietly. He looked at me when he was finished, saw me standing there with my fists clenched.

"So, you have anger," he said to me.

"Yes. Much anger," I said in Arapaho without thinking.

"You would fight the Ota?"

"I would kill the Ota."

"You would kill for the people?"

"Yes."

"Then, you are one of us, White Man. You are one of the people."

Realizing that I had spoken to One Dog in his own tongue, I went silent. I just glared at him, angry then at myself. Angry, not from giving myself away by speaking Arapaho, but angry at my confused feelings at that moment.

I was wondering, when the time came, if I could kill One Dog.

And if I did kill him, I wondered if I would have a guilty conscience.

Eight

The Ota had planned their ambush well. Two of the Arapaho braves who chased after them were killed soon afterward. From what I could gather after listening to the talk and deciphering the sign language, other Utes had been waiting for just such a move. As the riders rode down a narrow defile, Ota braves rose up on both sides and bombarded them with a cascade of arrows. One Arapaho had died instantly, I think, and the other bled to death on the ride back to where we were.

It was a bad day for the small band of Arapaho, and I grieved for the dead myself just as earlier I had grieved when the Ota had killed Walking Wolf. All the dead men were laid to rest on the scaffolds. I learned later that they were left there to avoid having their bones scattered by coyotes. The buzzards and worms would pick the bodies clean, but their skeletons would remain intact. One Arapaho boy told me they had learned this from the Crow people, who lived to the north. Some of the Arapaho apparently buried their dead just like we did, wrapping them in elk skins or deerskins instead of putting them in coffins.

One of the Arapaho braves retrieved the decoy pony, but when he tried to ride it, the pony turned up lame. One Dog told two of his warriors, Blue Cloud and Silver Rain, to kill it, and we ate horse meat while we continued to track the Utes through the rugged foothills. The Ota always seemed to be at least a day ahead of us.

Arguments began to break out among the Arapaho. Some of the braves wanted to go to the Sun Dance ceremony, but One Dog wanted his horses back and wanted to kill the Ota and take their women and ponies. The braves argued that their power was weak because they were not going to perform the Sun Dance. One Dog said that they were weak because they had let the Ota take away much of what they owned. It was clear to me that One Dog wanted revenge. All I wanted was to get my sister back.

A couple of days later, One Dog gathered his little band together and spoke to them.

"The summer grows short," he said. "Soon, it will be the Moon of the Changing Leaves. I know where the Ota goes. The Ota will also watch the sky and smell the wind. He will not go into the mountains. You women will take the children into the mountains to the place of the silver spring. You will wait there for us. The boys will make meat and you will sew the robes. You will wait for us. If we do not come before the first snow, we will return in the Moon of the Blackberries or the Moon of the Melting Snow."

No one protested. I sat there, listening, dumbfounded. One Dog was sending all the women and the children into the mountains, there to try to survive the snows and blizzards of winter. I wondered, and feared, what plans One Dog had for me.

"You have many years," One Dog said to me. "You are not a boy. You are a man. You will come with me and my braves. You will have a bow and a knife. But if you ever lift the bow or the knife against me or any of the people, you will die and your eyes will be cut out and your hands cut off. Your tongue will be cut from your mouth. You will wander the Star Path forever, unable to hunt or to see or to eat or speak."

"Why do you not let White Man go back to his people?"

"White Man goes where One Dog goes."

That was all he said, and I knew that, in his eyes, I was still a prisoner.

A young brave named Black Horse gave me a small bow, a quiver, and some arrows. These were not hunting arrows, but arrows used for killing men. He showed me the difference in the way the flint arrowhead was set in relation to the feathers. The killing arrowheads were placed so that they could penetrate between a man's ribs, parallel to the ground. The hunting arrows were so fashioned that they could penetrate an animal's chest, perpendicular to the ground.

Blue Cloud gave me a bone-handled knife that was also small, made in some white man's shop from a piece of thin iron ground to shape and sharpened on a grinding wheel. The quiver rode easily on my shoulder. It was unbeaded, so very unlike the fine quivers the Arapaho bore, but I was proud to have it, the bow, and the knife. These things made me feel like more of a man. But these tokens of manhood also bore a chilling message and a burden. With these lethal weapons, I knew I was expected to kill one or more of the

Ota. The message I garnered was: kill or be killed. And I knew I would not necessarily be killed by an Ota, but if I did not carry out my duties as a warrior, the Arapaho would see to it that I lost my life and my scalp.

I practiced shooting arrows every morning and night. Black Horse taught me how to draw an arrow quickly from my quiver and nock it to the gut string. Others taught me how to aim, the correct stance and proper angles of my arms. I became a pretty good shot in just a few days. Others taught me how to find water, seepage and springs. I carried one of the skin water bags, while other warriors traded off carrying our drinking water.

The Ota were clever at concealing their tracks. They would sometimes ride and walk single file. At other times, they split up, scattered like quail, and the Arapaho scouts had to figure out which track to follow. Sometimes, the Ota doubled back and we were forced to go into hiding. There were days when I felt Ota eyes on me, and when I told One Dog about it, he said that it was probably true. The Ota were watching us.

"Why do we not watch them?" I asked.

"Do you not see that some of our number are never near us?" One Dog asked.

I looked around and counted heads.

It was true. There were some braves who never seemed to join us, or came in at night and then left quickly.

"They are the watchers," One Dog said.

"How do they do this?"

"They are like the grass and the wind. They are like the shadow of the fir tree and the spruce, the pine and the juniper. They become the earth, the mouse, and the rabbit. They are the snake and the hawk on the limb of a pine tree. The Ota do not see them. The Ota do not hear them."

One Dog's words made the hairs on the back of my neck stand up and I could feel tiny spiders crawling up and down my spine. I looked around, wondering if the Ota could do such marvelous things.

"The Ota are like clumsy elk," One Dog said. "Their feet break dry branches. They stumble through the trees like old women. Pah."

"They sneaked up on us," I said.

"They put a crippled pony in our path and hid like children in the bushes."

One Dog had a point, but the way the Ota made their tracks slowed us down. Kate was getting farther away all the time, and I fretted that we seemed no closer to the Ota than before. I hunted the Ota with the Arapaho, but I was on foot and the Ota were on ponies. I felt like a tortoise trying to outrun a hare, which was a story I told One Dog. He laughed, enjoying the tale, then told me it was like one of the coyote stories the Arapaho like to tell.

A day later, following this conversation I had with One Dog, the two invisible scouts suddenly appeared. Their ponies looked tired, and I thought they must have come from a long way off. But that was not the case. The two braves, it turned out, had much to tell.

From the sign language they used and the few words I understood, they had seen a most remarkable sight and they could not wait for One Dog to come with them and read the sign on the ground.

These two braves were the watchers. Their names were Gray Snake and Little Blue Lizard.

"Many wagons come," Gray Snake said. "White men with many guns. Ota make friends with white eyes. White men have horses. They chase us away."

"The white eyes saw you?" One Dog said.

"They have the long eye," Little Blue Lizard said. From his signing, I knew he was talking about a telescope.

"Many white men. Many guns," Gray Snake said again.

"Let us go there and see what has happened," One Dog said.

It took us better than two hours to reach the spot where the two watchers had seen the white men in the wagons.

There were plenty of tracks, but none of them made any sense to me. One Dog waited before riding down to the plain where all the tracks crossed and crisscrossed on hard dry ground. He sent scouts into the hills to see if any Ota were there. When they came back, saying that the Ota had left, he led us all down to where the maze of tracks told a story he much wanted to read.

He made all the braves, save one, Gray Snake, stay away from the tracks. He and Gray Snake walked down and followed some. They bent over and pointed to significant tracks on the ground while I gritted my teeth, nervous as a long-tailed cat in a room full of rocking chairs.

Then, One Dog beckoned to me and I ran down to where he stood.

"You look," he said. "Read tracks."

He didn't point to any specific tracks, so I just looked at them. I could see the wagon ruts, and the hoofprints of shod horses. I also saw boot heels where white men had walked around. I saw some smudged footprints too, which I gathered were the moccasin tracks of the Ota who had come down to talk to the white men. I saw part of a cigarette ground into the dirt and what looked like specks of tobacco that had spilled.

I stopped looking, and I know I had a puzzled look on my face, because One Dog chuckled under his breath when he looked at me.

"What do your eyes see?" he asked.

I told him.

He grabbed my arm and drew me toward some wagon tracks. He pointed at some smudged tracks.

"Those your sister," he said.

My heart began to beat fast.

He pointed to more tracks that I could not decipher.

"White men trade for girls," he said.

"How do you know?"

"Tracks speak. Girls get inside wagon. Your sister go with white men. Ota ride away. They get guns, get tobacco."

He showed me where a rifle butt had been pressed into the ground.

"Kate gone?" I said, feeling stupid.

"Gone. Away. White men take. Take people girls too."

So, the Ota had traded Kate and the other two girls for guns and tobacco. I looked at the wagon tracks, followed them for as far as I could see. They headed south and away from the foothills, and disappeared at my limited horizon.

"We will follow the white man's wagons?" I asked.

"No. We follow Ota. We kill Ota. Get guns. Get tobacco."

My heart sank. Kate was being taken even farther away from me. I no longer cared about what happened to the Ota. I wanted to go and get my sister away from the white men who had bought her.

I wanted to tell them that I was her brother and that we had lost our parents to the Arapaho. I hoped they would treat us both kindly, but at the same time, my chest tightened and I had trouble drawing a good breath.

For some reason, a reason I could not clearly define, I thought Kate was now in more danger than she had been in before.

It was just a feeling, but I could feel fear clutching my heart in its cold black hand.

Nine

Much to my dismay, we followed the tracks of the Ota into the hills. For a long time, I could see the wagon tracks on the plain below and my heart ached to follow them, find Kate. Gray Snake and Little Blue Lizard evaporated into thin air. I wasn't even aware when they slipped away, but I knew they would soon find the Ota and turn invisible again.

It soon became evident to me that the Ota were following the same course as the white men, since they rode parallel to the wagon tracks. From where we were, I could still see the ruts and the hoof marks down on the plain. My heart began to beat rapidly, and I had to take deep breaths to calm myself, for I needed to plan ahead, and plan carefully, to make my escape from One Dog and the ever-watchful Arapaho braves. I also needed to find a boldness in myself to attempt such a thing. And as I looked inside myself that day, I knew I needed to find something else, something that I was sure I didn't possess.

Courage.

One Dog was not a stupid man. I thought he liked me, but I realized that was only my own perception, not his. He wanted me to teach him to read and write and talk English. Beyond that, he probably didn't care if I lived or died.

My hopes were dashed when we began to burrow deeper into the foothills and ascend even higher ridges. We soon left the wagon tracks and the plain behind. I did not know the West and I did not know where the white men were taking my sister, but I knew they had been headed south and I resolved one day to follow those tracks and find Kate.

I felt like a blind man as we headed into rougher country. The air was thinner, the trees thicker, but we were still roaming below the jagged high peaks that I saw on the skyline, their snowy tops glistening in the sun, their massive hulks a soft gray in the distance. They were ever present, ever elusive, just like those damned Ota.

Yet, I detected a change in One Dog soon after we went to higher ground. He was less talkative, more intense. I was burning with curiosity, so I asked him if the Ota were near.

"There is a place where they go that we know," he said.

"What is this place? Where is this place?"

One Dog merely pointed.

"Far?" I asked.

"Near."

Nearer than I would have guessed. The next morning Little Blue Lizard appeared out of the low clouds that seemed to have descended on us during the night. He looked haggard and tired. His eyes were red-rimmed and droopy, and he pointed to his moccasins. They were all worn on the soles from walking, yet he had ridden a horse. As I listened to him, I learned why his moccasins had turned to shreds of leather on his feet.

Lizard, in a few words and many signs from his hands, told a harrowing story of how the Ota had doubled back, chased him and Gray Snake, then forced them into a small box canyon, or steep ravine. I had to imagine most of it from Lizard's few words and his quick hand signs. The Ota had left two braves to guard the entrance. The Ota who were left behind carried the new Winchester repeating rifles. Lizard and Gray Snake waited until the sky ate the sun, then climbed out of the ravine, leaving their horses behind.

They snuck up behind the two Ota and killed them with their bare hands so that they would make no sounds for the other Ota to hear. Then they went back and got their horses. Gray Snake had the two rifles with him, for they had tracked the Ota to one of their sacred places. Gray Snake also had the two horses they had taken from the Ota they had killed.

One Dog was elated at this news, and we broke camp right away and followed Little Blue Lizard into the mountains. My chest burned from the pace Lizard was setting, and I was amazed at how tireless the Arapaho seemed to be. They trotted at a pace that looked easy, but my legs ached and my chest was on fire. In less than two hours, we came upon Gray Snake. I didn't see him right away for he was so well hidden in a copse of fir and spruce trees, just below a rocky ridge.

Sure enough, he had three ponies with him, and two Winchester rifles, a handful of cartridges. The rifles were just like those that Cassius Hogg had showed me and my father.

"I will look at the rifles," I told One Dog.

"Why will you look?"

"I may know the white man who gave the rifles to the Ota."

"You speak our tongue well," One Dog said.

"I listen."

"Good. You look at the rifles. Quick, quick. We must go. We must kill the Ota."

Gray Snake showed me the two rifles. Both looked brand-new, the bluing on them still shiny. My heart almost stopped when I looked at the mark on the barrel. When my father had dropped it, the barrel struck an exposed nail on the wagon. It had made the tiniest scratch, but Hogg had been angry about it. Now, as I looked at the metal scar, I could tell that someone had rubbed it with some material to dull it down so that the raw silver of the metal no longer showed through. But the mark was there, and it was the same rifle Hogg had shown us and that my father had accidentally dropped.

If Hogg had traded these rifles to the Utes, then he was nearby. And from the tracks and the accounts told by the Arapaho, there had been only one wagon. Where were the other two? What had happened to the families of David Prentiss and Giacomo Bandini? Had Hogg abandoned them to a fate similar to what had befallen me and my family?

I handed the rifles back to Gray Snake. One Dog took one, the one without the scratch.

"What do you see on the rifle?" he asked me.

"Nothing," I told him.

He didn't call me a liar right then and there, but I knew he didn't believe me. But he was in a hurry, and after giving the other braves a sign, we all followed Gray Snake. One Dog was now riding one of the Ota ponies and, to me, he looked tall and fierce.

We moved slowly and quietly through the pines, the spruce, the fir, and the juniper. The scent of the pines and the soft loam was heady in my nostrils, the fragrance almost a reminder of my dear mother, but oddly exhilarating because the essence of the aromas was something wild and savage. It was thrilling to me just to be with these strange men who were so at home in the wilderness, and I can only say that I felt then that I was closer to home than I'd ever been, closer to the feelings that lay buried deep in my heart, perhaps deep in my own ancestry. It's difficult to try and explain such a thing, but right then, I knew that I was no different from those savages around me. I was like them. They were like me.

It seems a man does not know who he really is, or where he comes from, or even where he is going, unless he somehow returns to his savage roots and discovers the savage inside himself, the wildness that has been there all along. And from that thought, another came to me. We, none of us knows what life is until we have faced death. When I killed the Ota, there was one moment when I felt something rise up in me, something that had been long hidden, and in that single moment, there was the feeling of eternity. There was fear too, but my own desire to live overcame that. No wonder such things are kept secret from us. That knowledge, bursting in on a man in one single moment that is eternal, is a terrible cross to bear.

I lost all track of time. I was caught up in the wonder of the woods and the mountains and the quiet men all around me who seemed to be part of the woods, like moving trees themselves, strange, almost mystical, dreamlike. But then, One Dog held up his hand and we all stopped, standing like statues, so like the trees around us, we might have been mistaken for them by animal or man. He made signals with his hands, and some of the braves slunk off in two directions as if they were encircling something I could not see.

Then, Little Blue Lizard touched my arm and put a finger to his lips when I looked at his face. He beckoned for me to follow him, which I did.

One Dog stepped down off his horse and tied it to a pine tree. So did the other mounted warriors.

It was very quiet.

One Dog, Lizard, and I hunched down like lowly beggars and walked straight forward. I could smell something then, something that stung my nostrils.

Smoke.

We were on a low grassy ridge stippled with wind-stunted pines and thick with brush. One Dog moved through the tangles with ease as Lizard and I followed.

There, below us, was the Ute camp. A small fire was blazing, and some of them had small animals on pointed sticks, cooking them over the fire. There was the smell of roasted meat, and my stomach roiled with a sudden splash of digestive juices.

One Dog signed for me to look at everything, really see what was to be seen down there.

One Ute was lying beneath a tree, on his back, an arm flung across his face as if he were asleep. Another stood at one edge of the small meadow, peering into the forest. Opposite him, on the other side, another brave stood watch.

The horses were hobbled in high grass at one corner of the flat, each nibbling, a sea of spotted hides that looked like a child's finger painting, the sort a man might paint when his mind was idling and he had only two or three colors on his palette, white, black, and brown, with perhaps a tinge of russet.

The fire burned beneath a spruce limb so that the smoke splattered against the needles and disappeared before it rose above the small valley. There were worn paths in several places, and a small brook, virtually noiseless, coursed through the center. High bluffs rose up on three sides, affording protection from attack in those directions. There was a narrow ravine just below the meadow's edge on one side, so that anyone riding up could be heard from some distance by those inside the small box canyon. I counted eight Ota, but there could have been more in the forest that rose up to the bluffs and beyond.

I nodded to One Dog. His lips parted in a brief smile, which he quickly extinguished.

The quiet rose up around me. Not so much as the chirp of a bird. I looked up at the sky, and saw an eagle floating high above the highest rimrock, silent, majestic, free, riding the air currents with outstretched wings.

Then I heard what I thought was a frog croak. My skin jumped. It was just a brief sound, but it startled me. I realized it had been voiced by One Dog. Such a simple sound, So innocent, so natural, in such a quiet setting.

My hair stood on end as One Dog and Lizard rose up and started shooting down at the Ota. In a blur, I saw the other Arapaho braves stream into the meadow from all sides. I saw both guards go down, with arrows jutting from their backs.

I scrambled down the slope, behind One Dog and Lizard, my heart lodged in my throat like a lump of lard. The high-pitched shrieks of the Arapaho tortured my eardrums and set my blood to boiling. Arrows flew all around and rifle shots reverberated off the bluff walls.

A Ute warrior rose up out of nowhere off to my right, and he had an arrow nocked to his bowstring. He was behind One Dog and Lizard, so they did not see him.

He stared at me and pulled the bowstring back to his ear. The arrow was pointed straight at me and my arrow was loose in my hand, my bow in the other.

The Ute was no more than twenty yards away.

Again, I faced eternity in that one single solitary moment when death stared straight into my very soul.

Ten

Something ticks in your mind.

Like a clock.

Tick, tick, tick.

You don't hear it, but your mind measures it. Sometimes there is only a half tick, or a quarter tick.

Then, when time is so measured, you know how much time you have to do a thing. To run, to kill, to save your life.

In that instant, when the Ute brave was pulling his arrow back to his ear, I could almost hear the string getting tight, growing tauter and tauter with each fraction of a second. And since I had no arrow nocked to my bowstring, or aimed at him, I made a decision that could have cost me my life.

Or it might have saved me.

Just before the Ute shot his arrow at me, I dropped my bow and arrow, lunged myself straight at him, and bent my back low to the ground. I ordered my feet to keep moving. The soles were hardened from walking in moccasins and the rocks beneath me didn't hurt at all. I scurried toward that Indian as I had seen quail scurry through the brush, moving my feet very fast as though I were working the treadle on a sewing machine.

As he loosed his arrow at me, I drew my knife from its scabbard, murder on my mind.

There was the whir-whiffle of the arrow as it passed over my head. My gaze was fixed on the Ute, my legs and feet working like pistons. The Ute made a big mistake then, and I felt a gloating warmth in my chest. Instead of bracing himself for my charge, or reaching for his knife or war club, he reached back over his shoulder to draw another war arrow from his quiver.

I raced even faster, my knife held low, pointed at him for an upward thrust. I ate up yards like a racehorse, closing the gap between us. Just as his fingers touched the fletching on his arrow, I leaped at him, pushing off from the ground with a mighty heave. The Ute's face seemed to turn pure white as the blood drained from it.

My body struck him full force. I reached up with my left hand to grab him by the throat. He fell backward under my weight and I tried to drive my knife into his side. But he squirmed like a slippery eel and bent his head backward, twisted it sideways. He struck the ground, with me on top of him. A rush of air exploded from his lungs. His foul breath bathed my face with its fetid odor.

The yelling and the cries of the other combatants turned dull and distant in my ears as I grappled with the Ute. His hands seemed to be all thumbs as they gouged at my eyes and throat. My right hand seemed fixed to a knife that was unusable. I struggled with my left arm and hand to subdue the Ute. He was short and stocky, but he seemed a bundle of muscles. I could feel his strength as I warded off those blinding thumbs, those gouging appendages that were attempting to put my lamp out.

He grunted as I dug my elbow into the hollow of his shoulder and brought up my right arm to plunge the knife in him. He turned his head and stared into my eyes. I cringed at the animal intensity of his gaze, the ferocity of the light that shone out of the blackness of those feral eyes.

I forced his head back and realized that I could draw my knife across his throat and end it. End him. So quick. So easy. So final. But something in me rebelled against cutting his throat. I don't know what it was, but I just could not part his flesh with the blade of my knife and watch his red life gush out like a crimson fountain. No, there was something too final about finishing him off that way. The man would have no time to reflect on his life or his god. I could not take that away from him. It seems stupid to me now. The man was trying to kill me, trying to wrest the knife from my hand, but I could not kill him in that way.

Instead, I jabbed the knife into his arm, the one that was fending me off. Blood squirted from the thin ragged wound and his grip did not loosen. I jerked my arm away from his grip and pushed on him. I rammed the blade of the knife into his side. It went in so easily and there was a hideous sound of the blade scraping against one of his ribs, the hiss of his flesh parting as it opened to the blade. My hand became drenched with blood and I pulled the knife out quickly, held it poised for another thrust.

The Ute shuddered and a sound escaped from his lips. It was not a gasp, but a word of some sort, perhaps the beginning of a final prayer. I do not know. But he twisted and turned back to me, and there was a knife in his right hand. He held it up as a priest might hold up a crucifix to ward off devils. It seemed a final act of defiance or duty, but when I saw the blade, an anger in me boiled over and I pounced on him, jabbing my knife into his belly until the smell of his intestines floated from the wounds and assailed my nostrils. He slashed weakly at me with his knife, and then I plunged my own into his chest, sliding the blade between ribs into his heart. He shuddered once and blood gushed from his mouth. His eyes closed and the animal light disappeared into the darkness of death.

I rose up from the Ute, panting for breath. My energy seemed spent, but I was strangely exhilarated, as if I had gotten a second wind. I drew in deep breaths and stepped back, looked down at the fallen brave with a mixture of complex feelings. There was blood on my hands and, looking at them, it seemed as if they belonged to someone else. Surely, those were not my hands, so saturated with blood, like a butcher's hands. I moved my fingers and discovered that they did indeed belong to me and no other.

My stomach fluttered and I began to visibly shake. The enormity of what I had just done gripped me and I had a bad case of buck fever. I turned away, my head swimming with giddiness. I walked back to my bow and the arrow I had dropped. It was automatic, that walk, done without reason or purpose. Later, I would become absorbed with that movement and come to believe that it was born of some survival mechanism inside me.

But it was silent in the meadow, except for odd sounds that I could not, or would not, identify. Whacking and cutting sounds. Animal grunts. Guttural whispers.

I picked up my bow and placed the arrow on it, then slid the nock onto the string as if I was ready to do battle once again. My giddiness vanished as my lungs filled with fresh air. Then I was swarmed over by Arapaho braves who had come up behind me. They slapped me on the back and nearly knocked me down. They went to the dead Ota and jabbed at him with their bows and rifles.

One Dog stayed with me, one of his arms draped over my shoulder.

"You have done well, White Man," he said. "You have taken the spirit of an enemy."

I said nothing.

"There is much food here. We will feast this night. Do you want the hair of the Ota you have killed?"

"No," I said.

One Dog spoke to Gray Snake. Gray Snake knelt down and, with his knife, made a circular cut on the scalp of the dead Ute. He lifted it from the dead man's head as easily as if he had just skinned a squirrel. My stomach revolted at the sight, but I kept everything inside by gulping in more air.

I was in a daze for several moments. My shakes had subsided with the touch of One Dog's arm on my shoulder. I did not dwell on what I had done, but I heard the others talking about my deed. At least one of them had seen the Ute rise up and point his arrow at me, and then had seen what I had done to avoid death. They all said that I was very brave for a white man.

A few moments later, I looked down at the body of Little Blue Lizard. He had been killed by an Ota. There was a small blue hole in his chest, from a bullet. He looked even younger in death than he had in life. I felt saddened by his death, almost as if he had been my own blood kin, a brother, or a cousin.

Gray Snake showed me the path to the bluff beyond the meadow. He showed me the outcroppings where the Ota had quarried flint for their knives and arrowheads. He

showed me the flat stones on which they had worked at
knapping, chipping off flakes of flint until the edges were
sharp and lethal.

I walked around that place and saw many broken arrowheads, picked up some to examine them. They looked like
pieces of velvet, and some were as black as ebony wood.
Some were covered with dirt and looked very old.

"Holy place," Gray Snake said. "Place where the Great
Spirit gave gifts to the Ota."

After that, standing below the towering bluff, I felt as if
I were in some kind of open-air chapel. I could almost feel
the reverence that the Ota must have felt when they came
there. Even Gray Snake seemed subdued and respectful.
And I noticed that he did not pick up any broken arrowheads or knife blades. Nor did he touch anything that was
there.

"Come," he said to me. "We go."

Little Blue Lizard was wrapped up and lying on a scaffold just inside the fringe of trees when Gray Snake and I
returned to the glade. One Dog stood by the little stream
that ran through the center, a stream that moved so slowly
it scarcely made a sound.

"Ota no sleep by water," One Dog said. "This water
good."

"Why do the Ota not sleep by water?"

"Noise. No hear enemy come."

"The Ota are wise then," I said, wondering if my words
would offend One Dog.

"In some things," he said.

We left that place, taking the food the Ota had stored
there. We stayed in the trees, though, which disappointed
me. I thought that now that we had bested the Ota, One

Dog would return to the plain where we could see the wagon tracks again.

The Arapaho seemed to know where they were going. We followed a game trail through the pines, past giant boulders and deadfalls lying in the solemn hush. Sunlight splayed golden shafts of light through the needles high in the trees, and we crossed through dark places where the sun was hidden. None of the Arapaho spoke, and we all had ponies to ride.

We came to an open place, a place protected by rocks and bluffs, in a low spot. There, we stopped and made camp. Some of the braves struck a fire and laid out Ota blankets and goods to admire them. I smelled meat cooking.

That night, each of the men spoke of his brave deeds that day. They acted them out around the fire so that each action was vivid and stark and clear by their movements. They all waited for me to stand up and recount what I had done. My face felt hot and I knew that I must be blushing. They teased me and called me a little girl. They called me a dumb white man. All of them were goading me to tell my story of blood and death.

"You talk," One Dog said.

I thought about what had happened that day. I could see the Ute rise up and take aim with his bow.

I spoke and told them what I saw.

Then I danced what had happened, forgetting where I was. I relived the fight, and the same emotions I had felt when I had killed the Ute came back to me. I became lost in the story, in the acting, the dancing. I pounced on the imaginary Ota and fought with his shade and plunged my knife into thin air, empty space.

I stopped and hung my head like an actor on stage about to take a bow in front of the curtain.

The Arapaho cheered me in their fashion and I sat down, strangely elated and satisfied in both body and spirit.

I looked around at all the men and at One Dog, their faces lit by firelight. That's when I knew what had happened to me without my even knowing it. These men had become like my own people. We were friends. I was one of them.

At that moment, I had become an Arapaho brave, bonded to them in blood and spirit.

Eleven

After a few days, it became clear that we were heading north. This was crushing news to me, since the wagon that had taken Kate had been heading south. When we came to the place where the women and children had gone, there was a jubilant reunion, and many of the young girls my own age began to regard me with more than passing interest. But I was thinking only of Kate, and now that I had a pony, my plans for escape became even more feasible.

One of the other young braves had died on our journey back. I hadn't realized that he was even wounded. His name was Mouse Whiskers. He carried an Ota arrowhead in his chest.

The arrow had gone in through his armpit, and he had broken off the shaft and told no one of the injury until the second day out, when we all stopped so that Mouse could sing his death song.

Mouse Whisker's body too was left to rot on a scaffold, and we rode on, ever northward.

"Why do you leave Lizard where we killed the Ota?" I asked One Dog, after leaving behind the dead body of Mouse Whiskers. "The other Ota will know who killed their men. They will hunt us and try to kill us."

"The Ota will know. If Little Blue Lizard does not tell them, our tracks will tell them."

"You want the Ota to know?"

"Yes," he said.

It seemed to me a strange way to live. Even though the Arapaho had exacted revenge on the marauding Ota who had first attacked them, it seemed to me it would have been wiser to have erased our tracks and let the Ota who discovered the bodies or skeletons of their brethren wonder who had killed them.

"Do you want war with the Ota?" I asked.

"The Ota is the enemy of the people. They steal from us. We steal from them. It has always been this way with the people."

The women of the Arapaho band fell upon the riches One Dog had brought back with him. Besides tobacco, salt, some flour, and beans, there were brightly colored beads of various sizes and shapes, and cloth, thread, needles with which to sew. Their delighted chatter floated to my ears, and I began to look at the faces of the women and the children. I had never really paid much attention to them before, blindly hating all of them for being associated with the murderers of my parents.

There was one woman who seemed to be the matriarch of the clan. All of the others deferred to her and asked her questions, always listening intently to her answers. Her name was Hisei Hiisiis, Sun Woman. Her eyes were as black as agates, and the wrinkles on her face were like the fine brushstrokes of an artist, deep furrows that seemed to tell a tale of her life and travails. Her face was round and small, the eyes deep-set, bordered by high smooth cheek-bones that were tinged with rouge, or vermilion. She had bad teeth and smoked a small clay pipe, giving her the look of a wise old philosopher.

The other women had similar faces, faces that seemed to tell the stories of their hard lives, but that was only my own perception and interpretation. The women, as the children, all seemed happy. Some of the women were pregnant, their bellies swollen beneath their deerskin and elk-skin garments, their faces glowing with the life of the child growing within them.

All of us hunted and brought back deer and elk that the women skinned and cut up for meat. We had brought back cooking pots and utensils that the Ota had once owned. It was clear to me that they had traded with the white men in the wagon for more than rifles, because the rifles, beads and cloth and thread, all seemed new. The women tanned the hides and were busy all the time, sewing beads on moccasins and dresses, leggings and shirts, washing, cooking, scraping hides that added to their riches.

A brave named Nech Nihaayaa', Yellow Water, befriended me one day after we had been out hunting and came back to camp empty-handed. The children were playing with sticks and rocks. The women were sitting in the shade, sewing moccasins and such. Yellow Water had some dried deerskins that had been rolled up, some little pots and things.

"Come," he said. "We make talk."

We walked over to the creek, where he laid out one of the skins and sat down. He began to place the little pots in a row next to the irregularly shaped, very thin, and soft skin. The other skins he left rolled up and out of his way.

Each little clay bowl had a substance in it. He pulled some sticks from inside his shirt. Tufts of hair had been glued or tied to the sticks. He mixed some sprinkles of creek water in the pots, stirred each one with the end of a different stick.

"You look, White Man," he said. "You see what Yellow Water makes."

He began to draw outlines of animals and men on the supple surface of the skin. He made these little stick figures with black dye or some kind of ink. He gave them bows and arrows, and rifles. He put them on horses and on foot. He did two rows of these on the top, and then painted some symbols that made no sense to me at the time. I watched him in fascination as he painted other figures in a fight with stick figures who were not on horses. He used red for blood and showed heads splitting open, arrows in chests. The tableau continued with depictions of scalping and mutilation.

I realized that Yellow Water was painting the fight in the meadow with the Ota. He even showed me plunging a knife into one of the men. He drew a symbol over my head to show that I was different from the Arapaho. It looked like a little white eye.

When he was finished, Yellow Water laid the painted skin in a patch of sunlight. He watched as I studied the drawing. It told the story, and it was interesting to me that its message dealt with men, with no attempt to depict where the fight took place. There were no landscape features whatsoever. It was all just flat and no sign of mountains or the meadow, the grass, the little creek that ran through it. It was odd, but my mind began filling in those spaces with descriptive words that I did not utter to Yellow Water. I supposed this came naturally to me since I read so much. I could still see that place so vividly in my mind and the painting gave me none of that feeling, as if the essence of the meadow had been omitted from the drawing. Yet, I had to admit, the stick figures did tell a grim and gruesome story.

"Do your eyes tell you what I drew?" he asked.

"Yes. It is the fight with the Ota."

He smiled.

"One Dog asks if you can put the talking scratches on the skin of the deer."

"One Dog wishes me to write the white man words on the skin of a deer?"

"He has spoken of this."

"Why? He does not read the scratchings of the white man's words."

Yellow Water jabbed a finger toward his painting.

"This I learned," he said, "from the Lakota, who have many such skins in their lodges. These pictures of the Lakota tell the stories of their people for many summers."

He spoke slowly, as if he wanted to make sure that I understood his words.

"The Lakota call these the 'winter count' and they are good to see. They are good stories of their people."

"So, you would make the drawings for the people and One Dog wants the white man words."

"That is so."

I considered what Yellow Water had told me, and I admit I was fascinated by the idea. Ever since I had lost my books and my writing paper, my fingers had itched to write down all that I had seen and learned.

Yellow Water pointed to the other rolled-up deerskins. He picked one up and handed it to me. I unrolled it and studied it. The leather was very soft and pliant. I had seen what Yellow Water had done with the brushes. Perhaps, I thought, I could modify them to make the hair thinner and actually write down letters of the alphabet, form words that would become sentences and paragraphs.

"I will do this," I said.

"Good. I go now. You make the scratches on the skin."

Yellow Water arose from the ground and walked away.

I picked up one of the brushes he had cleaned and studied how it was made. The hair looked to be from a mule deer. The strands were stiff until they were dipped in the dye or paint. If I could trim one of the brushes down and bring the strands to a point, I might be able to write with it, although I wished I had pencil and paper.

I had no idea why One Dog wanted such a record. Unless he planned to give them to a white man one day, it made no sense. But I knew that the Arapaho loved to tell stories and to listen to them. And this was not only a challenge, but an opportunity to test my writing skills and, perhaps, to teach One Dog a few more English words.

I took out my knife and began to trim the brush I held in my hand. I pared away the outer bristles and began to shape the brush so that it came to a point. I picked up the deerskin from my lap, then laid it flat on the ground. I made it as flat as I could and as stable as it could be on that piece of ground.

Then I dipped the tip of the brush into the pot with the black dye.

The writing would need a title, so I began with that at the top of the skin.

I wrote the title in capital letters thusly:

THE MEADOW FIGHT WITH THE OTA

I didn't know the Arapaho word for meadow, so I wiped out the title and wrote another one:

THE FIGHT IN THE GRASS WITH THE OTA

I realized that I was thinking in Arapaho as much as I was thinking in English. But I knew that I would have to read what I had written to One Dog.

Suddenly, I got excited about writing an account of the battle.

I would make it simple and clear. I would choose each word carefully from a small vocabulary that could be easily translated into the Arapaho tongue. Images began to form in my mind. And I had Yellow Water's drawing to look at for not only my inspiration, but for the flow of the story. I would embellish it, of course, and make One Dog the main character, the hero.

I thought of the words I would put down and when I had enough courage, I began to write, slowly and carefully forming each letter. Time lost its grip on me as I entered another world, the world of imagination and creativity. I drew my inspiration from the pictures in my mind and from Yellow Water's skimpy stick figures.

In my mind, I wasn't just writing a little story about a battle between two warring tribes. I was writing an epic, a smaller version of the *Odyssey* or the *Iliad*.

I was creating a myth from my own time and experience perhaps, just as Homer had done many thousands of years ago.

I began to write:

I speak of a great man, One Dog, and the great men of the people. I speak of bows and arrows and rifles and the bad hearts of the Ota.

I was writing in the English language, but I was telling the story the way Homer might have told it if he had been speaking in Arapaho to the Arapaho on a dark evening when the fire threw skulking shadows on the wall of a cave and the people sat around, listening intently to the immortal words written on the soft skin of a deer.

Twelve

My body became brown that summer and my hair grew
long. If you had seen me with the Arapaho, you would
have thought we were all of the same blood. When I saw
my reflection in a lake one morning, I jumped back, thinking someone else was in the water, coming straight at me.
No, not just someone else, a savage Indian whom I did not
recognize.

I knew that my birthday had passed, in June, but I didn't
know the day or date, since the Arapaho didn't keep any
calendar that I could understand. It didn't seem to matter
anyway. I had turned eighteen, grown an inch or two taller,
and a young pretty girl named Blue Owl braided my hair. It
took her some time, and the touch of her fingers on my bare
shoulders not only soothed me, but conveyed some of the
affection I had missed from my mother and my sister.

I didn't know how old Blue Owl was, but she told me
how she got her name.

"When my mother gave light to me," she said, "the sun was unborn. The little owl called from a tree. My mother saw the owl. It was blue because the light in the sky was small. To my mother, the owl looked blue."

"It's a pretty name," I said.

"I do not like your name."

"My name is Jared. Jare Edd."

She twisted my name in her mouth, but it was hard for her to pronounce.

"The name One Dog gave you, I mean to say," she said.

"White Man."

"Yes. That name. It is an ugly name."

"My other name is Sundown."

She could pronounce that one.

"What does Sundown mean?" she asked.

"Before the sky eats the sun," I told her, "it sits above the land. When it falls and you do not see it anymore, but it brings light to the clouds, that is sundown in our language."

"That is a pretty name," she said. "I will call you Sundown."

The words she used in Arapaho were not an exact translation, but meant something like Sun Gone or "The sun has been eaten by the sky." It was a mouthful to say and she laughed when I told her so, so she just shortened it to Sun and made a sign that showed it had sunk over the horizon.

One Dog liked the story I wrote about the fight in the meadow. He liked being the hero of the story and bragged about it to anyone who would listen. Which gave me an idea.

I knew that the Arapaho would soon leave to hunt buffalo again before they went to winter quarters on the prairie. The herds, they complained, were small and hard to find since the white eyes had shot most of them, left their bodies to rot in the sun. The Arapaho were bitter about the decimation of the great buffalo herds that had once thundered across the prairie like an endless river.

I was going to escape, but I wanted to set matters straight before I left. And I hoped I would not have to kill One Dog or any of the other braves, some of whom I liked and found to be pretty good companions at times. But I needed to enlist the artist, Yellow Water, to help me with my project.

Three of the women had given birth that summer, and one of them was the wife of Yellow Water, a woman named something like Bad Temper. She was aptly named, for she had a scathing, scolding tongue and was constantly berating her husband or ordering him about as if he were her personal slave. Yellow Water was quite docile under such tongue-lashings, but I knew he was not happy to be around her.

"Yellow Water," I said to him one day, "I would like you to make a painting for me. It is to be a gift for One Dog. Will you make this painting for me?"

He was suspicious.

"What do you wish me to paint?"

"A story."

"What story? You do not know the story of the people."

"This is a story about my father and the two young boys who hunted the antelope and were killed by the long rifles."

"That is not a good story."

"It is a true story," I told him.

Yellow Water said that he would think about it, and he moped around for a couple of days while his wife chastised him for everything he had done or hadn't done and should have done to make her happy.

Finally, Yellow Water came to me with some tanned deer hides, his paint bowls, and brushes and said that we would go to the creek.

"If I do not like the story you wish me to paint, I will beat you up," he told me.

"One Dog will like the story. You do not have to like it."

"If I paint it," he said, "I will have to like the story. It must be a good story."

"It is a good story. It is a true story."

"So your mouth speaks, White Man."

We sat down and Yellow Water laid out a skin and dipped his brushes in water and then into the bowls.

"Draw an antelope," I told him.

I had him draw the two boys, lying on their backs, their legs lifted like the blades of a scissors. He drew in the bows and arrows. Then I had him draw two white men with rifles. These were depicted as being on horseback.

I asked Yellow Water to draw a scene showing the two white men taking the scalps of the two boys after they had shot them. Then, for a final panel, I had him draw a wagon showing the men putting the scalps inside the wagon. Beside the wagon, but looking the other way, I had him draw a white man and woman with two children, a boy and a girl. Over the boy's head I told him to draw a white eye.

"Why do you ask me to draw this eye?"

"Because that is my sign," I told him.

"What do you say to me, White Man?"

"I say that another man killed the two boys of your people and put the scalps inside the wagon of my father so that he would take the blame for the kill. My father did not kill the two young men of your people."

"Ah. So, this is why you have me draw this story?"

"Yes. It is the truth."

"One Dog will not like this story."

"I do not care if One Dog likes the story. But I am going to make the scratches that tell him this true story, Yellow Water. You go now. Leave the skins and the paints and the brushes."

He got up and looked at me. I had never seen pity in an Arapaho's eyes, but the look in Yellow Water's appeared to be something mighty close to pity, the kind of pity one might extend to an imbecilic child.

"It does not matter," he said.

"What does not matter?"

"That your father did not kill the two boys of our people."

"Why not?"

"What one does, all do. Your father was of the tribe of white eyes."

I did not know if the Arapaho had a word for justice. If they did, I had never heard it. But I wanted to cry out to Yellow Water that my father and mother deserved justice. Instead, I looked at Yellow Water and told him this:

"My mother never killed anything. She never killed the rabbit, nor the mouse, nor the fly."

"What one does, all do."

There was no pity in Yellow Water's eyes. Contempt perhaps, or an age-old hatred of white men that I had stirred up. He walked away, his back as straight as a fence post. I took another skin and began to write the story of that day when Hogg and Rudy Truitt had killed those two Arapaho boys and scalped them. I wrote short easy sentences that followed the tableau that Yellow Water had drawn on the other skin.

I wrote that my father's heart was filled with sorrow when he saw what Hogg and Truitt had done and that he had been banished from the tribe, left to wander like the Arapaho people, exiled like Odysseus, forced to find his way to a home far to the west where the sun set, where it dropped burning into the sea. With a flourish, I wrote the last line.

"That place where the sun dies in the water, and the water turns red and dark as wine."

Homer, I thought, would have been proud of what I wrote that day.

I returned the brushes and the pots of dye to Yellow Water's lodge, a lean-to covered with spruce branches, and then went to see One Dog. He was sitting under a tree near his lean-to, chipping flakes from a piece of flint.

I gave One Dog the painting and showed him the other skin with the white man's scratches on it.

"What is this you give me, White Man?"

"It is a story. The story of who killed those two boys. I have written it down in white man's words. If you wish, I will read it to you, tell you its meaning."

He put down the flint and the rock he was using to knap the stone into a sharp arrowhead.

He studied Yellow Water's drawings, grunting as the story unfolded.

"I see you and your sister," he said.

"Yes. We did not want the bad white man to kill those two boys. We turned our backs on him."

"But you were of the same tribe?"

"No. We gave the man the shining yellow metal to take us across the land of your people. He stole from us. He put the scalps in our wagon. He wanted you to kill us."

"Why did he do this?"

"Because he is a bad white man. I think he is the same man who gave rifles to the Ota. I think he bought the girls from the Ota."

"Ha. You do not know this."

"No, but one of the rifles belonged to this bad white man. It is the rifle with the wound on it, a wound my father made when he dropped it from his hands."

"Read me the story. I will see if I can make sense of it," One Dog said.

I read him the story. It was very short. I read it very slowly, hoping he would understand most of the white man's words.

When I finished, he asked me to tell him the story in his own language.

I did that, wondering if I was using the correct words.

When I finished, One Dog was silent for a long time. He got up, went to his lean-to, and came back with a pipe filled with tobacco. He used the burning glass to light his pipe. He held the glass up to the sun so that one ray struck the tobacco and turned it hot, set it on fire. He smoked, looking at me with no expression on his face.

"What you say to me may be true," he said. "But the world is the way the world is. I cannot change it. You cannot change it. Your father is gone. Your mother is gone. You are here. You are alive. Your sister is somewhere else. Maybe she is alive too. You have all that you need. I cannot bring your father and your mother back. They are gone to the setting sun, the sun you say that falls into the sea and drowns. Do not speak of this to me ever again."

"Yes, One Dog. I have spoken. So it will be. What one does, all do."

"What? You give blame to your father and mother?"

"What one does, all do."

He gave me a stern look. I got up and walked away, leaving him there. I knew he was mad, but I didn't care.

I wanted One Dog to think over my words. If I had written them well and spoken them well, they would be like little burrowing worms, gnawing away at his primitive Arapaho mind. They would consume him from within, perhaps make him question his own beliefs.

Then, perhaps, the Arapaho might come up with a word that meant justice.

I thought that, but I knew it would never be so.

One Dog was One Dog, and he could not be anything else. He acted according to his nature, as all people do.

But I wanted him to know that I blamed him and his whole tribe for the murder of my parents, the loss of my sister.

What one does, all do.

Thirteen

We changed camps many times that summer. The women were kept busy tanning deer and elk hides, sewing teepees, cutting up meat, curing it, and cooking it over small fires that concealed our smoke. I was beginning to realize that the Arapaho were a constantly hunted people. Their numbers, I learned, had diminished considerably since the advent of the white man, which included Spaniards, Frenchmen, and Americans.

But, as some told me, mainly Blue Owl, who shared my buffalo robe at night, the Arapaho were always a scattered people, homeless by our standards, but actually sharing lands with other tribes as long as the other tribes didn't know they were around. They had come from the north, Blue Owl told me, but their legends went all the way back to the beginning of creation. These tales, she said, were too sacred for her to share with me, but she hoped that someday, the tribe would accept me and I would hear these ancient stories of how the people came to be.

We hunted buffalo on the plain one last time that summer, and when we left the mountains for the plain, we had travois and teepees and buffalo robes for the winter. We traveled south and east to a large river that I later learned was called the South Platte. The Arapaho didn't call it that, however. They called it the Musselshell and sometimes at night, when the light from the moon was on the water, I thought I could see little shells in the lapping waves. Long ago, Blue Owl told me, the people used to gather mussels there, or they saw mussel shells washed up by some long-ago or faraway sea.

I was still planning my escape now that I had my own pony, but the Arapaho were subtly clever. I was never left alone, yet, for all outward appearances, none of the braves behaved like guards or watchers. They were very clever, I decided. And sometimes, I thought, they could read my thoughts. But then, I have to admit, I gave them good reason to suspect that I might run away from them.

One day I asked Yellow Water if he knew what lay to the south of the Musselshell.

"Why do you ask this?"

"I am as curious as an antelope," I said.

"When the antelope is curious, he falls to the arrow."

"Tell me, if you know. But I think you do not know the land to the south."

"I know it."

"You have been there? No, you could not have gone to the south. The people would not let one so young go to unknown land."

"I have been there. I have seen the white man forts and the white man towns."

"Can you draw them for me? In the dirt?"

"I can draw them."

"I do not think that you can. I think you are making it up that you have been to the south."

Yellow Water got angry with me, but he plunked down on his loinclothed butt and picked up a stick. He began to draw furiously in the soft earth, rivers, trails, forts, and towns.

"Do you know the names of these places?" I asked him.

He shook his head. But I kept the map in my mind, and later came to know the names of Fort Collins, Pueblo, Taos, and Santa Fe. And the rivers were the South Platte, the Cache la Poudre, and El Rio Grande del Norte. But I was not to know these names or hear them mentioned for some time yet, and I didn't realize how long I would remain with the Arapaho.

We did cross wagon tracks on our way to the Mussel-shell, but the Arapaho stayed well away from traveled roads and trails. They were furtive without appearing to be so. I knew better than to ask any of the tribe about these roads. I just kept their images and locations in my mind.

Dogs came to the new camp. These were thin, rangy dogs, ribs showing like slats through their mangy hides. The Arapaho appeared to have known them, or the dogs knew the Arapaho, because the animals came in, one by one, wagging their tails, and the people fed them and petted them. These dogs were ridden with fleas and soon I saw the children scratching. So I stayed well away from the dogs. But the children hooked them up to little play travois and had a fine time playing with them.

From where we camped, I saw the first snows of the mountains. It started snowing up in the Rockies during the night and by morning, all of the dark faces of the mountains were white and beautiful. The air was chill and we had snows too, bad ones, drifting ones, but the fires in the teepees kept us warm and there was plenty of food.

Blue Owl pestered me that first winter with the Arapaho.

"Why you no give me baby?" she said, using the English I had taught her. It was then I realized why she kept asking me the words she wanted to learn, especially the word "baby."

"We are not married," I said.

"What is 'married'?"

I realized that I had stepped into a linguistic tangle. There was no such word that I knew of in the Arapaho tongue, and our customs were just too complicated for Blue Owl to understand. But I tried to explain it to her.

"The white man has a dance he does with a woman," I lamely explained. "There is a medicine man, a shaman, who speaks words over them. The man and woman give each other rings. They put these rings on their fingers and then the shaman 'marries' them. It is a treaty the shaman makes with the Great Spirit. He asks the Great Spirit to make this man and woman into one spirit, a human spirit, so that they may live together always."

"You give me ring," she said.

"I do not have a ring to give you."

"You give me ring," she insisted.

When Blue Owl and I made love, I always pulled out before spilling my seed in her. I knew that much about the birds and bees, but not much else. She always urged me to stay inside her, but I didn't want her to have my child. So there were constant arguments and she accused me of being less than a man.

But I set out to make her a ring. And, of course, I had to make one for myself.

We did not have any gold or silver, or at least I didn't, so I thought I would make the rings from an elk antler I had. The antler had broken off, but was long enough to be used as a back-scratcher and that was its use to me. I knew that I could cut up the antler, with a lot of sawing with my knife, and this is what I did. I cut two round pieces from the antler, one large enough for my ring finger, and a smaller one for Blue Owl.

It was difficult work, but I cut these two circular chunks from the antler and then began hollowing them out with the tip of my knife blade. I expected the task would take me some time, perhaps all winter, and I was in no hurry. As long as Blue Owl saw me working on the rings, she seemed content not to pester me.

It snowed fairly often that winter down on the Musselshell, which made the tracking of game easier and more fun. I got to be a pretty good shot with a bow, but I had my eye on a muzzle-loading rifle that one of the braves owned, a man named Speckled Hawk. I knew I would never get my hands on one of the Winchesters, and even if I did, I'd be hard-pressed to steal ammunition for it. But I remembered that first lake where the Arapaho had taken me and Kate and all the powder, ball, and other things I had hidden there. And I had a pretty good idea where it was, since through all of our journeys, I had been keeping a map in my head. I studied that map on many a night when I was gazing up at the stars. In fact, I transferred that map to the heavens and found the constellations that fit it. So, whenever I got the chance to ride away from my captors, I could just look up at the night sky and follow my map.

The rifle was Pennsylvania-made, from a place called Lancaster. Speckled Hawk let me look at it one day when I asked him. I didn't just ask him outright, because that was not the Arapaho way. Instead, I told him I admired it and thought it was a fine rifle. I told him I wondered if it shot true and if he had ever missed with it. He told me that he had not, that it was a very good rifle and shot truer than any he had ever owned. He said his father had gotten it from an old white man who trapped in the mountains. He said that his father had coveted the rifle and one day, when he had the chance, he had killed the white man and taken his rifle. When Speckled Hawk's father died, he inherited the rifle and all the possibles that went with it, a ball pouch, a mold to make the lead balls, a powder flask, and good flints. He cut little pieces of leather to hold the flints in the vise.

I told Speckled Hawk that my father had owned such a flintlock rifle, but that it was not nearly so good and had been converted to percussion. He wanted to know what percussion was, and I told him about the little copper caps that exploded when the hammer struck them. This fascinated Speckled Hawk, and he said that he would like to own such a rifle so that he would not have to make flints anymore.

So, I examined the rifle. I held it to my shoulder and liked the fit of the stock to my shoulder. The stock was made of curly maple and was quite beautiful. It had a patch box of copper inlaid into the stock near the butt, and a fine hickory ramrod with brass fittings. The rifle was in .64 caliber and with one hundred grains of powder could knock a buffalo bull down with one shot.

This was a beautiful long rifle, much nicer than the one my father had owned, and I had no doubt that it shot true. I vowed to myself that when I made my escape, I would steal the rifle from Speckled Hawk, just as his father had stolen it from an old mountain man long ago.

But after that day when I looked at the rifle, Speckled Hawk and others kept their eyes on me more intently than ever.

I felt as if the Arapaho could truly read my thoughts.

Much as I yearned to make my escape that winter, the red men of One Dog's tribe never gave me the chance.

I was still a prisoner.

And I pined for my sister Kate on those long winter nights when snow flocked the land and locked it into a deafening silence, broken only by the howl of a wolf sounding as lonely as I was, and just as lost.

Fourteen

One cold winter day, it must have been February or March, two white hunters on horseback stopped by the Arapaho camp on the Musselshell. I had been sprouting hair on my face, much to my embarrassment, and had taken to scraping the silky strands off with the blade of my knife. I was well embedded in the tribe and did not want to appear different. My skin was tanned from wind and sun, and my single braid had grown long until it was halfway down my back.

The two men of my race looked hard-bitten, but it was obvious that they were acquainted with One Dog and several of the braves. They were greeted warmly and offered the hospitality of the band. They were leading two pack mules. They spoke a little Arapaho, but mostly spoke in hand sign, or in French, of which I knew very little. But I stayed close to One Dog, who invited them grandly into his teepee.

"You make the hunt," One Dog said, using sign language.

"Oui," one of the men said. "We hunt the elk for the fort."

One Dog called this man "Pierre," although his pronunciation was not the best. I learned his name from the other man, whom One Dog called "Jock." I knew his name was Jacques, because the two men used each other's names and pronounced them correctly.

"There are few of your people left on the plains," Pierre said as he smoked the long pipe that One Dog passed around after he lit it. "It is the same everywhere we go. The white eyes do not want the Indian people riding around loose, hunting the buffalo, killing the game."

"This land is of the people," One Dog said.

"Soldiers might shoot you," Jacques said. "The white eyes want to put you in a camp of their own making so that they can watch you."

"They hunt the people, these soldiers?" One Dog said.

"Yes," Pierre told him, then he looked at me.

"Your son, One Dog?" he said.

"No. He is a slave."

"What tribe is he?" Jacques asked.

One Dog laughed.

"I'm an American," I said, just blurting it out.

Both Frenchmen drew back in surprise, their faces alight with astonishment.

"Oh, an *american,*" Pierre said. *"C'est bon."*

"Do you know a man named Hogg?" I asked.

The two men looked at each other, their eyebrows rising like caterpillars.

"He is your father?" Jacques said.

"No. I am wondering if you have seen this man with a young white girl named Kate."

"We know this man," Pierre said. "He is a very bad man. He sells guns to the Indians, and whiskey."

"What about the white girl?" I persisted.

"He come into the fort with some girls," Jacques said. "Two Indian girls and a white girl. I think her name was Kate."

"What did he do with her?"

"He sold the white girl," Jacques said. "He said that she was a bond servant."

"Who bought her?"

"What was the name of that farmer, Pierre? Petti-bone, no?"

"Pettigrew, I think. Yes, Pettigrew. I do not know his given name."

"Enough white man talk," One Dog said, interrupting.

I wanted to talk more with these men, but One Dog scowled at me and the two Frenchmen deferred to his authority.

Pierre and Jacques stayed the night, then left early the next morning before I got the chance to talk to them again. But I had a name. Pettigrew. I knew where I might find Kate if I could ever escape from the Arapaho. I was excited, so I went to One Dog that day and came right out with it.

"One Dog, will you hear me?" I said.

"Speak."

"I would like to go to the fort and look for my sister."

He didn't answer right away, and I was somewhat encouraged by his silence. When he did speak, he dashed my hopes to the ground and trampled on them as if they were pests.

"You are no more a white man," he said. "You belong to the people. We are your tribe now. Do not go to the white man's fort. They will put you in a cage like a wild animal. They might kill you. Do you not see yourself? You are one of us now."

"I am still me."

"Yes, you are you. But you are one of the people. You are of my tribe."

"I want to see my sister."

"What of the two girls of our people who were stolen by the Ota and taken by this white man? Do you not think we want to see them too?"

"Yes. I could find them for you."

"No. Not at the white man's fort. You will not go there. To the people, those girls are dead. To you, your sister must be dead. That is what your thoughts must say to you. Then you will live as you should live, with your people. This is your place. This is my place."

I wanted to kill One Dog right then and there. I wanted to curse him for being a liar. Kate was not dead. And those two Arapaho girls were probably alive, working for some farmer, like Kate was. I couldn't understand the logic of One Dog when he said that we must consider those girls dead. If he would pursue and attack the Ota who took them, why would he not do the same with the white men who bought them from the Ota? I could not argue with him. He walked away from me, and I knew that I had to keep my thoughts to myself from that moment on. But I would have those thoughts. One Dog could not control those. He might hold me prisoner, but my thoughts roamed free as the eagle flying high in the sky.

I figured that the fort the two French hunters were talking about was the one to the south of the Medicine Bow mountain range. They had called it Fort Collins. I figured they might pass through the Arapaho camp again on their way back, packing elk meat on their mules.

So I used Yellow Water's paints and wrote a letter to Kate on a piece of tanned deer hide. I lied to him and said

I was writing something for One Dog, who was out hunting that day. When I finished the letter, I hid it under my buffalo blanket that I slept on at night. When I left the teepee, I kept the letter inside my elk-skin shirt so that One Dog would not find it in case he got suspicious and started searching through my bed when I was away from the teepee.

Here is what I wrote:

Dear Kate, I am alive. I will come for you one day. Be strong. Wait for me. Your loving brother, Jared

I didn't know if my letter had any chance of reaching her, even if I could give it to one of the hunters. But I had hope and that was one of the things that kept me alive, kept me scheming and planning to run away from the Arapaho and find my sister.

The two French hunters did return, twice more that winter. When they rode up, I made sure I was within earshot.

"Look, Pierre," I said quickly, "I've got a letter written on deerskin that I'd like you to take back to Fort Collins with you. It's to my sister, Kate, and maybe you can find someone who knows Pettigrew and can see that she gets it."

"You ask much, son," Pierre said. "What is your name? One Dog said he called you White Man."

"My name is Jared Sunnedon. Just think of Sundown if you have trouble remembering it. I don't want One Dog to know about this."

"Where is this letter?"

"In my teepee. Are you staying the night?"

"Just the night," Pierre said. "And we shall return once we deliver the meat to the fort."

"I'll get the letter to you. Later."

"Good."

One Dog walked up and I had to stop talking. My heart was in my throat, squeezed tighter than a fist.

I was a little surprised when Jacques walked out of the teepee after eating. He had a lit pipe in his mouth. It was a cool evening, but the snow had melted. He was dressed in buckskin and had a buffalo jacket on, so he was not cold.

"Pierre and One Dog are talking inside," he said. "I will smoke the pipe and talk to you, Sundown."

"I have the letter inside my shirt," I said. "Do you want me to give it to you? Then you can give it to Pierre."

"I will take it," he said.

I had the letter rolled up and tucked inside my trousers under my shirt. I slipped it out and handed it to Jacques. He quickly put it inside his shirt, out of sight.

"Thank you," I said.

"The fort, she is a busy place. The people, they come and they go. We do not know this Pettigrew, but we have heard his name. It is a large family, I think. From what I have heard of them. We will keep our eyes and ears open, but we will not be there long. We hunt again very soon."

"Even if you give the letter to someone who knows the Pettigrews. Just be sure that Cassius Hogg does not know about it. He is the reason I am a prisoner of the Arapaho."

"The Arapaho, they are a fine people. But One Dog would not like it if you tried to run away. He might kill you."

"I know."

"So, what do you do? You become an Arapaho? It is not a bad life."

"No, it's a good life. But I miss my own kind, sir."

Jacques laughed.

"You are better off with the Arapaho," he said.

We spoke no more that night. The next morning, he and

Pierre were gone, and when they left it felt as if a part of my heart had been torn away and they had taken it with them. I missed Kate so much. I missed speaking English.

I missed my parents and the life we might have had in Oregon.

And I did not want to become an Arapaho and live with them the rest of my life.

But I realized that I was already an Arapaho, and watching those two men leave was like being stranded on an island all alone and watching the last boat sail away into the morning sun.

Fifteen

One Dog moved our camp, much to my dismay. I was
hoping to get some news from Pierre and Jacques when
they returned from Fort Collins. I kept wondering if One
Dog moved us deliberately so that I would not see them
again. I fretted for days at the new digs on the Musselshell,
trying not to show my displeasure. To calm my nerves and
take my mind off of this latest disappointment, I worked on
the two rings I was carving out of the elk antler. I had the
insides nearly hollowed out, and planned to do a great deal
of smoothing so that there would be no sharp edges when
they were finished.

You could feel spring coming. And there was much talk
of it among the women and children. The men turned rest-
less and they talked of the changing weather and watched
the sky every day. One night, we held a council of all the
men. One Dog spoke to us all.

"The elk herd will be coming back," he said. "On the
next sun, we will ride to the place of the two rivers and

watch for them. We will find much meat. We will hear the birds singing. We will see the arrows in the sky and hear the geese at night."

The next day, we struck the camp, hooked up the travois, folded the teepees. Everyone pitched in and it did not take long. It was still very cold, but I could feel a change in the weather. Warm winds blew off the prairie. The mountains were still white as far as you could see, and there was ice along the shores of the Musselshell.

I felt a tingling excitement as we moved southward. I was trying to figure out where this place was that One Dog had talked about, "the place of the two rivers." I was reading the maps in my mind and could see the marks Yellow Water had made in the dirt, showing the forts and towns. And the rivers. There was a place just north of Fort Collins where a river joined what I took to be the South Platte, the Musselshell. My heart beat faster knowing we would be near where I believed Kate to be.

The scouts ranged far and wide as we traveled southward. We saw a lot of scattered elk tracks, but not so many as to indicate a large herd. I was confident that the Arapaho knew of their migrations, however, and this place we were going to would surely see the return of the elk herd to the foothills, if not the mountains themselves. I felt the excitement of the other tribe members too. The women and children all seemed as if they were going to a fair or a picnic. They were chattering all the time, and the women would scrape the thin mantle of snow looking for signs of grass seeds sprouting.

We camped some distance from the river, but not too far away that we couldn't walk to it. I went with One Dog and the other braves to scout the place where the elk herd might pass by, and that's when I saw the two rivers One Dog had mentioned. I learned from Yellow Water that the little river that flowed into the South Platte was called by the French Cache la Poudre. It was a place where the French trappers had cached their traps and furs, apparently when the fur trade was at its highest. The Arapaho had several names for the river, none of which seemed to stick for very long. But Yellow Water called it the River of Many Stones, saying that he had been up it once, hunting, but had been chased back down by a band of Ota.

It was still cold, and it snowed very heavily one night and for most of the next day. I worked on the two antler rings and shivered next to the fire. The snow did not melt right away, and the weather stayed very cold for a couple of weeks. Then, gradually, the snow began to melt and young men went outside and put their heads to the ground, listening for the thunder of hoofbeats that would tell them when the elk herd was returning.

We saw one or two elk venturing toward the confluence of the two rivers. One Dog let them pass by, waiting for the rest of the herd to come in as the days grew warmer.

More and more elk began to appear, and then we heard shots farther south, downriver. One Dog, Yellow Water, a few other braves, and I went to investigate. We rode along the river, the braves looking down at the ground, checking for sign. We rode very slowly, just in case we might come upon a large herd of elk.

Then we heard two sharp rifle shots from far away downriver.

One Dog called a halt, as if there was something different about these shots. And when I reflected upon it during those moments, there *was* something different about them, something ominous. Those two shots would ring in my ears for many years afterward, as it turned out.

"Who will ride to the sound of the rifles and be my eyes?" One Dog asked.

"I will go there," Yellow Water said.

"Go. We will follow."

Several minutes later, Yellow Water returned.

"Come see," he said. He made the sign with his hands that spoke of two dead men. White eyes.

There were a lot of tracks around the bodies. Two men lay close together, their heads clotting with blood. Each had a bullet hole in the back of the head. Their faces were distorted because the bullets had blown off their foreheads. And they had both been scalped. But I knew from their clothing who they were.

Pierre and Jacques.

One Dog and the others read the tracks while I stared at the two men lying there in the thinning snow, their faces all but obliterated. It was hard to take, having known them as strong men, eating, breathing, talking. Two bullets in the backs of their heads. My first thought was that they had been ambushed by Ota, or some other tribe.

"Ota?" I asked One Dog.

"No Ota. White eyes killed these two. My friends."

"But their scalps were taken."

"White man cut head, take hair," he said. "You look tracks. See boots. Tracks tell story."

Yellow Water pointed to some hoofprints.

"Mule," he said. "Two mule."

"Their pack mules," I said in English.

"Shoot men, take mules, ride away." Yellow Water gestured to the south, toward Fort Collins. I looked at the tracks and followed one set. Two men had killed the Frenchmen. I found where they had sat their shod horses and probably shot Pierre and Jacques. I rode their tracks back to the scene of the murders. I saw the tracks where the Frenchmen had come out of the foothills. Part of a butchered elk lay there, its head. The mule tracks were deep, showing that the mules had been loaded with meat.

I went over the maze of tracks, pieced together the story as I could understand it. The other braves and One Dog were doing the same. Each Arapaho might have his own interpretation of what had happened, and I would have mine. Those two men were waiting for the Frenchmen, waiting to steal from them. They had shot them, scalped them to make it look like the work of Indians, and then taken the pack mules and ridden back to the fort with their booty, their ill-gotten gains.

I dismounted and looked at the bodies. Their rifles and pistols were gone too. They still wore their knives. I wondered if Yellow Water had scared the killers off. It looked that way.

I went through their pockets and was glad that I did. They both had currency on them, paper money and coins.

The Arapaho were not interested in the money, so I set it aside on the ground. Then I felt something crinkle when I touched it. It was in a pocket of Pierre's shirt. Paper. But not flimsy like the money I had found. I pulled it out. It was a single piece of paper, folded over. Someone had poured candle wax on the place where the folds came together so that it would not open by itself.

I turned the paper over in my hands.

There was writing on it.

When I read the words, my heart jumped.

To Jared Sunnedon.

My hands began to shake as I pulled at the paper to break the seal. There was too much wax on the fold. I took out my knife and ran the blade through the wax. The sealed part opened. With trembling hands, I opened all of it and saw the familiar writing. It was a letter from my sister, Kate.

Dear Jared, the letter began.

I am sending this with the man who gave me your letter and told me about you. I am living with a family as their bond servant. They bought me from Mr. Hogg. My master is Amos Pettigrew. He is a farmer. We are leaving soon and going north to a place called Laramie, I think. I am glad you are alive. If you come, you may be able to buy me from Mr. Pettigrew. He is a very mean man. I can't say much more. I hope you can find me. I love you, Jared, and cry for you every night.

Kate had signed the letter.

"What do you have there?" One Dog asked as I stood up, the paper in my hands shaking like an aspen leaf in the wind.

"It is writing. From my sister."

"She lives then?"

"Yes, she lives. She is a slave."

One Dog smiled. "Good. She is where she is."

"What do you mean by that?" I asked.

He gave a slight shrug. "We are who we are."

"She is not a slave."

"You said that she was."

"I mean that she is a captive."

"Then, that too. That is her fate."

That was the first time One Dog had ever used that word to me. I knew what the word was because Blue Owl had used it and told me what it meant.

"She waits for me," I said, trying to hold down my anger.

"Then, that is her fate too, White Man. To wait."

"Let me go, One Dog. Let me find my sister."

"No," he said. "You have a different fate. Your fate is with the people."

I cursed One Dog under my breath. I wanted to strike him dead on the spot. Some of the braves were looking at me. All were armed. If I so much as raised a hand toward One Dog, they would cut me down like a stalk of corn.

"Yes," I said, trying to put timidity in my voice.

"Good. You good man."

I was in a daze for some time. The big herd of elk had not passed that way, but we found several tracks and we saw where the Frenchmen had killed elk, butchered them, and packed them on their mules.

I wondered who had killed them.

I had a pretty good idea who the two men were.

Hogg and Truitt.

Someday, I thought, I'd call them out for all they had done.

But first, I had to escape the Arapaho.

Somehow, I had to change my fate.

Sixteen

It was late afternoon on a warm sunny day when the elk herd began to drift into the foothills. Scouts, with ears to the ground, had heard the gentle thud of their hooves as they walked off the plain. We were all well hidden and the breeze was blowing toward us, so the elk could not see or hear us. We were all armed with bows and arrows. There were braves up above us and on both sides of the canyon where the Cache la Poudre flowed toward the South Platte.

The women had kept all the dogs in camp, so they had not followed us. Our ponies were tied up, out of sight.

Most of us were hidden in sight of shallow water, around a couple of bends. Above the bend, the water was swift and I could hear its roar as it came down the steep canyon. But this was a wide place where the elk could go to drink. And they would all be out in the open, within easy range of our bows.

I took four arrows from my quiver, laid three of them out on the ground within easy reach, and nocked the fourth one on my bowstring. Elk drifted up the canyon in twos and threes, some singles. Some stopped at the first easy place to drink, but others kept on going. More and more elk began to appear. I started to shake with excitement. There were some yearlings among the herd, but many were large animals. The bulls had huge antlers and they looked dangerous.

The elk were wary, but none of the Arapaho moved and neither did I. Finally, I heard, from quite a ways upstream, the whiffle of an arrow, followed by a soft *whump*. I saw a bull elk stagger and go down. Then, both sides of the canyon filled with flying arrows.

I picked out a cow that was about twenty yards from me. She had stopped and I had a clear shot at her heart, just behind her right leg. I took aim, held my breath, and loosed the arrow. It thunked into her and she took off at a run. I thought for a moment that I had missed hitting her heart, but as she crashed through the shallow water, I saw blood streaming from her wound. She ran about fifty yards, then dropped, skidding through the shallows. Her chest stopped heaving and she lay still, dead as a stone.

I quickly nocked another arrow. By now, some of the herd had started to run up the trail next to the Poudre. Arrows flew from both sides. Elk dropped in their tracks or ran on, wounded, only to fall later. I shot a small bull, missed the vital part, and penetrated its stomach. I felt sick and put another arrow to my string. The elk was turning in circles, blood streaming from its wound. I drew my bow, took aim, and shot it again, the arrow ramming in just behind its right shoulder blade, into the lung. It coughed and struggled to stay on its feet. Pieces of white lung matter came out of its mouth along with a great deal of blood. It went to a deeper part of the river and fell into it, then wallowed there for a good five minutes. It tried to rise again, and fell down for the last time.

The herd began to run upriver, and soon only the fallen elk were left behind. Arapaho emerged from their hiding places and checked the fallen elk, cutting the throats of those still alive. Two braves rode off to fetch the women and children, ponies and travois. From the looks of it, I knew they would be butchering all day. I checked the last elk I had dropped and determined that it was dead. The cold water had stopped the bleeding before it died apparently, but my arrow had punctured a lung. It must have bled to death, but I knew the shock of that arrow with the weight of the shaft behind the arrowhead was powerful. The Arapaho had told me that the animals felt no pain when they began to die. I wasn't so sure.

I walked down to the smallest elk I'd killed. I pulled the carcass up on the shore, slit it open, and removed the heart. I knew some of the Arapaho were watching me, so I was determined to put on a good show for them. I ate the warm heart, letting the blood run down my chin and onto my chest. I made grunting sounds and pounded my chest to show that I had taken on the power of the elk. My stomach rebelled against the raw meat, but I held it down. I removed the liver from the same elk and tucked the meat into my shirt, stuffed it under the sash I was wearing.

Soon, the women and children arrived and there was great rejoicing among them. The children had a field day running from elk to elk and striking coups on them with their sticks, howling like a pack of banshees until the canyon rang with their cries.

For a time I felt like part of the tribe, but my mind was on Kate's letter. If I didn't get away soon, she would go up north and be farther away.

And I got to thinking about those boot tracks around the bodies of the two Frenchmen. The more I thought of them, the more familiar they seemed. Back when my folks were still alive and we were still a family, I was sure I had seen those same boot tracks. But at that time, I never even thought of tracking. Since being with the Arapaho, I had learned to be more observant of everything. One Dog had made me lie down and study a patch of grass for almost a whole day. He told me to remember everything I saw and then tell him that night.

At first, I thought it was a stupid thing to do. It didn't make any sense to me. Then, as I lay there on my belly, watching the grass and the dirt, I began to see things. Small things. Tiny things. I saw the grass move when a bug crawled along a blade, climbing to the top to snip off the tip. I saw ants and small insects moving through the dirt and over it. I soon lost track of the big world and became absorbed in the miniature realm that existed on that small chunk of soil. I felt like a giant in a kingdom of small creatures.

I became aware of every tuft and sniff of breeze. I saw what the wind did to the grass and I saw ants toiling, traveling back and forth across the patch, sometimes carrying a piece of a dead worm on their backs. I noticed that they went to a place unfettered and each came back with a portion of a dead worm or a bug. One ant reminded me of a man lugging a huge grand piano on his back. It kept staggering and dropping the dead bug, only to persist and pick it up again, continuing on its way.

I saw a universe in miniature that day, and when one of the braves walked across that same piece of ground, I opened my mouth to yell at him in admonition. He was destroying my world. I looked up at him, ready to berate him. He walked on past and said, "Look. You will see."

I watched the way the grass flattened under his moccasins and then watched as it slowly sprung back, marveling at its resilience. I looked at every crushed blade and saw them each move back to their former shape. Like magic. I saw flying insects land and take off. I saw one ant tribe make war on another. I saw little bugs burrowing beneath the soil and emerging somewhere else. A mouse even picked its way through, and I saw what effect his passing had on the grass, and I pushed up to see the tiny, almost invisible, tracks he left in the dirt.

When I spoke to One Dog that night and told him all that I had seen, he seemed pleased.

"There is more," he said.

"But I saw much."

"There is always more, White Man."

And he made me do it again. And again.

"This is what the tracking man must know," One Dog told me. "He must know all of the world he sees and the world he does not see."

Gradually, I began to understand what One Dog meant. I did see more, and I began to piece together the small lives that lived underfoot. In doing so, I gained more respect for all living things.

This was why I was puzzling over those boot tracks that I saw. I knew that I had seen them before. I just had to remember and then I had to trust my memory. One Dog had told me a thing that I have not forgotten.

"Your memory must be as clear as those words you scratch on the deerskin. It must remain like the pictures Yellow Water draws. You must be able to see through the running water of the creek and count the little stones and know each one."

I began to practice my memory because One Dog was

always testing me. When we would ride on the hunt, he would ask me what I had seen along a particular stretch. He made me name the trees and tell about the kind of bark they had. He would ask me about rock formations and the way the land rose and fell. I would have to name landmarks, both large and small, and if I made a mistake, he would tell me that I had the eyes of an old blind woman.

I roamed back through my memory as a white boy before I had ever seen an Indian. And I saw those same boot tracks around the fire, by the wagons. I saw where men had gone to take a piss or where they squatted and made grunt. I saw all those things through the haze of memory and they became clear and vivid to me, as if they had happened yesterday.

Hogg. One of those sets of boot tracks belonged to Cassius Hogg. And the other might as well have had the man's name written on it in big block letters. Rudy Truitt. Those were the two men who had murdered Pierre and Jacques. I was sure of it now. Perhaps it had been a small suspicion in my mind, but it was no longer. I knew, without a doubt, that Hogg and Truitt had ambushed the Frenchmen, killed and robbed them.

The hatred for those two men began to build inside me. I think I was hating them more than I had once thought I hated One Dog. Hogg and Truitt were the source of all the troubles that had befallen Kate and me, my folks. They had been the ones who killed and scalped the two Arapaho boys, for no reason, and then Hogg had laid the blame on our pa. He had banished us from his wagon train; he had turned us into exiles and kept our money. In looking back, I realized that what he did that day might have saved Kate's and my lives, since I suspicioned that he might have done away with the Prentisses and the Bandinis as well.

He sure as hell hadn't taken them to Oregon. And probably not even to Santa Fe.

As we rode back to camp that night, the travois full of fresh meat and elk hides, I had much to mull over. As exhilarating as the hunt had been, I knew that I would never be completely happy living as an Arapaho. Maybe if Kate had still been with us, I might have felt a lot differently about it. Maybe. There are journeys we never take, and we always wonder what might have happened at that fork in the road if we had taken one path instead of another. But we can't go back. We can't correct our mistakes, or carry regrets for what we might have done but didn't do.

Kate was alive. She was living with a white family, but I knew, reading between the lines of her letter, that she was not happy. She had said that Amos Pettigrew was a mean man. I knew Kate. She would never have said that unless it were true, and knowing her, I was sure that Mr. Pettigrew was more than mean to her. She always looked at bad people more kindly than I did, probably because of her feminine nature and the fact that she was more like our ma.

There was jubilance among the Arapaho that night and for several days thereafter. The weather turned warmer each day, and I knew it must be April or perhaps May. I did not have a calendar and the Arapaho did not mark each day as white people did. Time meant little to them. They spoke of a sun as being a day and they spoke of years. But they never spoke of moments or hours or centuries. Time was a fluid thing that they recognized and accepted, but made no special mention of beyond noticing the seasons and the months. One year was much like the next, without any special number or name to it unless some great event had happened.

But for me, time was now a gnawing animal in my

mind. Like a giant rat, it was eating me from the inside out. I thought of an hourglass set with its full side up, and I could feel and see the grains of sand seeping through the hole and filling up the bottom half.

Time and the Arapaho were my enemy, and I had to find a way to conquer each one and set out to find my sister Kate.

The falling sands seemed to be speeding up, and I had no idea where the Arapaho would go next. I lived in dread that we would go into the mountains and not come out until the Moon of the Falling Leaves.

And where would Kate be by then?

I resolved to escape before One Dog gave the order to leave the Musselshell. We were so near Fort Collins now and this was my best chance. But how could I escape and take that rifle I so wanted?

That was a question I had to answer.

Soon.

Seventeen

Fate, the mysterious and elusive thread that wove through a man's life, that controlled his destiny perhaps, occupied my thoughts at the end of that winter. Homer's heroes, the people in his stories, were controlled by Fate and the gods controlled Fate. I felt like Odysseus tossed upon an unknown sea, the winds driving me toward an unknown port. But Odysseus had fought against Fate, and so would I. I did not believe in Homer's gods, but the Arapaho, and One Dog, most surely did. If man has gods directing him along life's path, I reasoned, let's see whose gods are more powerful, mine or the Arapaho's. The great heroes controlled their own fates. I hoped I could find the same courage.

As luck would have it, Fate did play a hand in certain future events. Luck or Fate? Both were intangibles, hard to pin down. Although I was a dreamer, I was also a determined man.

A few days after the elk hunt was over, when the Arapaho were feeling fat and sassy, with full bellies, plenty of meat, and spring well on its way, a party of traders descended on our camp along the Musselshell.

The leader of the party was a jovial man named Ormly House. He was tall, thin as a rail, with curly locks and a full beard. With him was a cadre of fellow adventurers, all grown men, drovers by trade, all with wagons. They had four wagons and two men to a wagon, with extra horses besides those that pulled the wagons, two to a wagon. They spoke the lingua franca of the plains, sign language, and said they had been with the Crow and the Lakota and were headed for Santa Fe.

They had goods to trade and wanted some buffalo robes and elk hides to sell in Santa Fe. One Dog seemed pleased to have visitors, even if they were white men. And the women of the tribe were like a flock of clucking chickens when the traders laid out their blankets and covered them with beads, silk cloth, mirrors, trinkets, and all sorts of gewgaws.

Ormly came over to me and looked me square in the eyes.

"You ain't no redskin," he said. "Though your skin's plumb near burnt to a bacon crisp."

"No, sir. I'm an American."

"What you doin' with these red niggers, son?"

"I'm a captive, sir."

"A captive? Well, what the hell? You want to come with us to Santa Fe?"

"I surely would like to do that, mister. But I don't think One Dog will sell me to you."

Ormly laughed. Uproariously.

"Hell, I ain't goin' to buy you, sonny. I'm just sayin' you can come along with us, if you want."

"You'll have to talk to One Dog."

"He the big chief of this outfit?"

"I guess so."

"I reckon you'll have to do the talkin'. I don't speak Rappyhoe none. You know, you look plumb Injun, 'ceptin' for them blue eyes."

"I've got to get away from these Arapaho. Maybe you and your men could jump them and . . ."

He held up both his hands and backed away from me.

"No, siree sir, not this child. We wipe out this band and we'd have the whole Rappyhoe nation down on our asses. You got troubles, son, you solve 'em your own self. I seen enough scalpin' in my day."

I glared at him, but I knew I had failed to gain an ally. Ormly would be no help to me. I started wondering if I could hide out in one of the wagons before they left and maybe hitch a ride without anyone knowing.

The women and braves bargained for the goods the traders had laid out. Ormly and his men wanted some of the elk meat, and there was plenty to give them, and they wanted skins and buffalo hides, which the Arapaho were reluctant to part with, but the trading went on, with both sides wrangling for the best deal.

At the end of the trading, when there was just one fine buffalo hide left on the blanket, one of Ormly's bunch went to the wagon and brought out a large wooden box.

"Firewater," he said, setting the box down next to the buffalo hide. "For the robe."

One Dog's eyes widened.

He reached in and pulled one of the bottles from the box. He shook it and the sun struck the contents, making the liquid glow like amber.

"Go ahead," Ormly said. "Take yourself a swaller." He made a sign of tilting the bottle up.

One Dog pulled the cork out with his teeth and poured whiskey down his gullet. A lot of it. His eyes watered with tears and he shook with the power of it.

"Good whiskey," One Dog said in English.

Then he pointed to the buffalo hide.

"You take," One Dog said. "Me take whiskey."

Ormly grinned. He nodded to one of the men, who swooped in and snatched up the heavy robe and staggered off toward one of the wagons.

The Arapaho braves began to clamor for the whiskey, and One Dog started passing out the bottles.

"Thank you, Chief," Ormly said, rising up from his squat on the ground. "We'll be passin' on then."

One Dog waved Ormly away and took another swig of the whiskey. He grinned at Ormly and that was all.

I walked over to Ormly.

"Do you think that was right, giving these Indians whiskey?"

"What's your name?" he asked.

"Jared Sunnedon. Sundown."

"Sundown, whiskey's what them red niggers thrive on. It makes them feel real big. But you want some advice?"

"If it's good advice."

"Them Injuns'll get real rotten drunk tonight, and if you ever got a chance to light a shuck, that would be the time."

"Can you do me a favor, Ormly?"

"I might."

"Down the trail, where the two rivers meet, could you leave me some powder and ball in .64 caliber?"

He grinned wide.

"You aimin' to do it, ain't ye? Well, I reckon we can leave you a cache. Them's the South Platte and the Poudre yonder. I'll pile some rocks up over the powder and ball, so's you can find it. That all?"

"I can't pay you."

"Maybe someday we'll meet under brighter circumstances, Sundown. You can pay me then."

"Yes, sir," I said.

He touched the brim of his hat and climbed up on his horse.

"Good-bye," I said.

"So long, Sundown. Watch your hair."

He laughed, raised a hand, and let it fall. The wagons rumbled off behind him. I watched them until they disappeared over the horizon. When I turned back, the Arapaho women were fighting over the goods they had bought and the men were all sitting around in a circle, sipping the whiskey, talking about how good the firewater was in their bellies.

I had never seen Indians drink whiskey. I didn't even know that the Arapaho knew what it was until that day. But I had seen men come out of the taverns back in Missouri, drunk and staggering, sometimes fighting with each other. Pa had always abstained from strong drink, and he often warned me about its effect on men. He never told me not to drink, but advised me that if I ever did drink whiskey, to take it only in moderation.

The way the Arapaho were going at it, it didn't look much like moderation to me.

Yellow Water lifted his head and saw me. He gestured for me to come over and join them. Then One Dog looked at me and beckoned for me. So did some of the others. I walked over and sat down next to Yellow Water and Black Horse. All of the men were grinning like a bunch of empty-headed yokels.

"Drink," One Dog said.

Yellow Water handed me the bottle he had in his hand. All of the men told me to drink. I upended the bottle and pressed my lips together so that only a small amount would enter my mouth. I pretended to drink a swallow or two, but let only a trickle pass my lips.

I handed the bottle back to Yellow Water and wiped my hand across my lips. He slapped me on the back and all of the others grunted their approval.

The whiskey seeped down my throat. It warmed me. Then it reached my stomach and I felt the fire of it. It made me feel a little giddy, and I knew that if I drank any more I would get drunk and lose what few senses I still had.

I sat there and pretended to drink when a bottle was handed to me. The men drank a lot, and one or two got up, staggered away, and vomited. Then they came back for more. Some began to brag about how brave they were, how many coups they had counted, how many men they had killed.

I got up after a while, and nobody seemed to care. They were all busy drinking and bragging.

I walked around, checked the pony herd to see which boys were guarding them. They paid me little mind, and I walked back to my teepee and sat outside as the shadows of afternoon grew long. I kept my eyes on Speckled Hawk, whose eyes had turned red and were beginning to glaze.

Some of the women begged for whiskey, and One Dog let each of them drink some, whacking one on the butt as she trotted away, giggling to herself. The men got up, stretched, pissed, and sat down again to drink more whiskey. The women cooked the meat and made their husbands come and eat. As night fell, most of the men had eaten and then had gone back to drinking more whiskey. I ate and waited, watching.

While the Indians were getting drunk, I gathered a few things and put them in a pouch with a sling. These were things I might need later on if I was able to run away without being shot dead. I got flint and steel, a burning glass, and some dried jerked elk meat. Some I stole from One Dog's teepee. The jerky was in my own teepee, kept there by Blue Owl. I hid the pouch outside my teepee, under a loose flap of hide.

Ormly had been right, I thought. This just might be my opportunity to escape from the Arapaho. When One Dog called me back over, I sat down, pretending to be a little drunk. He handed me a bottle and, again, I pretended to swallow a lot. I did get more than I wanted in my mouth, and then let it trickle down my throat very slowly. I pretended to get drunker. Gradually, I began to act like they did, muttering and mumbling, slurring my Arapaho words. One Dog smiled drunkenly at me.

I didn't think the whiskey would last long at the rate the men were consuming it. But they were not drinking so much as the evening wore on. A couple of men got up and went to their teepees, carrying their bottles with them. I heard them crash to their blankets and figured they had passed out.

I kept my eyes on Speckled Hawk, who seemed to have an iron constitution. But the whiskey got to him too, and he arose and made several attempts to align himself up with his teepee. I knew that he was not married and lived alone. It took him a few seconds to navigate to his teepee, and a few more to overcome the perversity of an inanimate object, namely, the tent flap. Finally, he went inside and I heard him fall to his bed.

One Dog hardly noticed me when he staggered to his feet. I helped him inside his teepee and helped him into his bed. He lay on his back, eyes closed, and began to snore loudly. I waited, holding my breath, my heart pounding. The little amount of whiskey I had consumed helped give me courage. But I was still afraid.

I was going to make my move, but I knew that if I made even one small mistake, someone in the tribe would kill me and never even bat an eye.

I got up and walked out into the night. Billions of stars twinkled overhead and the camp was quiet. Even the dogs were asleep. I took a deep breath to clear my head, and then started my stealthy walk toward the teepee of Speckled Hawk.

I knew it would be dark inside and I would have to find his rifle by using my hands, careful not to awaken him.

I would be as a blind man, not only tempting Fate, but trying to change my own.

Fate was a hell of a thing to be thinking of at that time, but there it was. In my mind. Huge, formidable, dangerous.

I listened outside the tent flap for a few minutes, then ducked down and stepped inside, into the darkness. Into the unknown.

Eighteen

Speckled Hawk was snoring, and I knew he was dead asleep as I crept inside his teepee. I did not know where he kept his flintlock rifle. The only light came from the stars shining through the smoke hole above me. The light was very faint and I could not make out objects. But I knew where Speckled Hawk was, and I moved around the wall of the teepee, groping ahead of me, feeling the ground with my moccasined feet.

I made one circuit without finding what I was looking for. So I walked another circle, closer to the center. I stretched a foot out and felt before I made a step. Finally, I stubbed my toe on something hard. I reached down and picked it up. I felt it with my hands. It was a war club. I stuck it in my sash. I would need that when I went to get my pony out of the herd. If any of the boys were awake and challenged me, I would brain him to silence.

Every small sound I made sent an alarm shooting through

my senses. I took my time, feeling with my feet. I kept shortening my circles, careful not to disturb the sleeping man. On the last step of the final circuit, my toe touched something soft. I put my foot on it and it gave way, but there were hard things inside. I reached down and felt it with my hand. It was, I decided, Speckled Hawk's hunting pouch, with powder, ball, mold, grease, and patches inside. I picked it up and slung it over my shoulder.

But where in hell was his rifle?

I had gone over every inch of the dirt floor of the teepee. Had I missed a spot? I didn't think so. I got down on my hands and knees and started feeling around on top of the buffalo robe, on both sides of Speckled Hawk. Finally, as I was about to give up and brain the sleeping man so I could feel underneath the buffalo hide, I felt the stock of the rifle. The brass butt plate was cool to my touch. My heart leaped in my chest, or it felt like that, and I slid my hand along the stock until I felt the trigger guard and the lock. I gently picked up the rifle and scooted backward, away from the robe. I picked up the rifle, my heart pounding fast, barely able to breath.

Then Speckled Hawk stopped snoring. My heart stopped too. I froze and waited, my hand gripping the handle of the war club. He turned over, and every nerve in my body jangled like a sack full of cowbells. I felt like screaming against the fear and the darkness.

The snoring began again and I slipped outside the teepee, letting out a long sigh of relief.

The rifle felt good in my hands. It had a long octagonal barrel and was heavy, but it gave me both comfort and courage to be holding it in my hand. I hefted it as if to make sure I still had it, then let it drop back down. I started toward my own teepee to pick up my pouch. A dog slunk past me and my heart skipped a beat. In the distance, a wolf howled. This was followed by a series of coyote yelps that ranged up and down the musical scale.

As I was reaching down for my pouch, I heard the soft whisper of moccasins behind me. I felt a hand touch my back. The touch was gentle, but I knew it was a human hand.

"Sundown," she whispered.

I picked up the pouch and stood up, turned around.

"What do you do?" Blue Owl whispered.

"I go."

"Come into the teepee with me."

She touched my arm, clasped it with gentle fingers, pleading for me to follow her.

"Come," she said, and I felt my will cave in, collapse inside me.

I followed her into our teepee, mostly because I did not want to cause a ruckus outside.

"Where do you go?" she asked, her voice still a soft whisper.

"To the white man's fort south of the two rivers."

"I go with you."

"No."

"Yes," she said. "I am your wife."

She opened my hand and placed something in it, then closed it up again.

"What did you put in my hand?"

"Look," she said.

I opened my hand and looked.

I could barely see what she had put there, but there was enough starlight from the smoke hole for me to see the objects. I felt them with my other hand to make sure.

"Oh, Blue Owl," I said.

She had put the two unfinished rings in my hand. They were almost finished. They could be worn, though, as they were.

"You make promise to Blue Owl," she said.

There was disappointment in her voice and it made me suddenly sad. I had promised. But I had not planned on taking Blue Owl with me. That would only anger One Dog more than my own escape would infuriate him.

"You go with me?" I croaked, my throat so constricted I could barely get the words out past my lips.

"Where Sundown goes, Blue Owl goes."

"There is much danger."

"I know. I go with you."

"Does your heart say this?"

"My heart and my head, they say this."

I was touched. But I was also annoyed. I hadn't planned for this. Now my escape was fraught with even more peril. I didn't even know if she could ride a pony. Would I have to carry her on my little pony, slowing us down?

"Can you ride a pony?" I asked.

"I can ride the pony."

"You must be quiet."

"We go now?" she said.

"Yes. Come."

"Wait," she said. She took the rings out of my hand. She put the big one on my finger and the small one on hers. Then she walked over to a corner of the teepee and picked up something. I couldn't see what it was until she came back with it. She slung a pouch over her shoulder.

"I have food," she said.

We stole out of our teepee, went outside the camp circle, and headed toward the pony herd downriver, perhaps three or four hundred yards away.

As we got closer to the ponies, we could hear them huffing as they grazed. I wondered if the flintlock was loaded as I looked for the boys on watch. But even if it was, I would only get one shot and we'd be caught. Still, I hoped it was loaded and that there was powder in the pan.

Blue Owl had better eyesight in the dark than I did. She reached out an arm to stop me, then pointed to something dark on the ground. I looked at her and she made the sign for sleeping. I nodded and we went on, making little sound with our moccasins.

Blue Owl stopped me again and pointed in another direction. Again, a black lumpy shape on the ground. Another boy, asleep.

We got close to the herd. The ponies made no sound, but continued eating grass. Some lifted their heads to look at us. Blue Owl stopped again, reached inside the large pouch she had on her shoulder, and took out a bridle. I took my bridle out of my pouch. We grinned at each other in the dark.

We separated to look for the ponies we wanted. I moved through the grazing herd, straining my eyes to pick out my own pony. Finally, I saw him, near the middle of the herd, and crept toward him, hoping he would not spook. He let me come up to him and I patted his neck, then slipped the bridle over his head, my heart pounding like a kettledrum.

I untied the hobble around his forelegs, then climbed on his back. I hunched over so that I would not present my silhouette to anyone who might be watching. I looked around for Blue Owl, but didn't see her.

Slowly, I eased the pony through the herd, out to the very edge. I looked up at the stars, found the polestar in the Big Dipper, and then glanced at the river, shining silver in the moonlight.

I had a plan to throw trackers off my trail, but we had to get well away from the Arapaho camp before it could be executed. I waited impatiently for Blue Owl, wondering if she was going to betray me and give the alarm that would foil my escape. I wasn't very trusting at that moment. It was all looking too damned easy.

Finally, I heard a faint sound and then saw a pony drifting my way. At first I thought it was just a lone pony moving slowly to a different grazing spot, hindered by its hobbles. I saw the darker shape clinging to its back and breathed in, grateful that she was not going to give us away.

I pointed to the river and Blue Owl shook her head. She pointed away from the river, then signed for me to follow her. I felt that I had no choice, so I did what she asked.

She rode away from the river, but headed southward. We both moved so slowly, I thought we'd never get away from the herd. I thought that at any moment one or both of those boys would wake up and start raising a ruckus.

Coyotes yapped and sang somewhere out on the prairie, and the silence after their chorus died down was both a blessing and a curse.

Sound carried a long way on such a clear night, and to me, the sound of the ponies' hooves sounded like thunder, even though their footfalls with unshod hooves were soft and muffled. The river vanished and when I looked back, so had the horse herd. It seemed as if it had taken us hours to ride only a few yards. I expected a horde of Arapaho, drunken Arapaho at that, to come chasing after us, yelling war cries and murderous threats.

We rode on, putting distance between us and the camp. I started ticking off time in my mind, white man's time, and an hour went by. Then another. And I was lost. There were no landmarks, no river to guide me southward. I tilted my head and gazed up at the stars. They blurred from the sweat that had dripped into my eyes. I was wringing wet from perspiration, even though the evening was very cool. My nerves rippled like fingers plucking harp strings. How far had we come? Were we out of immediate danger? Thoughts skidded off my mind like water in a hot skillet.

I wiped my eyes and looked up at the Big Dipper again. It seemed to me we were heading east as I checked every few minutes over the next hour of riding so slowly. It felt as if we were treading through quicksand.

Blue Owl turned her pony to the west, angling away from our course, back toward the river.

"Do you know where we are?" I asked her.

"River close. We cross."

It was close. The South Platte rose up like a ribbon sprinkled with diamonds. I don't know how Blue Owl knew where to go, but she did. We rode up to a shallow ford in a wide bend and trotted our ponies across. We let them drink on the other side, then continued southward.

I began to relax.

It looked as if we had made our escape. I murmured a silent prayer of thanks to the Great Spirit and to my own God, and all the gods of the Greeks.

When we stopped, I checked my newly acquired flintlock. I ran the wiping stick down the barrel and listened to the thunk against a lead ball. I opened the frizzen and checked the pan, holding the rifle up and tilting it toward the feeble light from the moon. I thought I could see a faint patina of powder. So Speckled Hawk kept the rifle loaded and primed. Good man.

We rode all night, crossed the river twice more at fords. I was amazed at Blue Owl's strength and courage. She was leaving her own people to be with me and that made my heart swell with pride. I did not think, then, of the effect we'd have on the good white citizens of Fort Collins when we landed in their midst.

Had I been able to look into the future, I just might have turned back right then and there.

Nineteen

Blue Owl and I were a tribe that night. A tribe of two.

We rode into the pines and spruce and firs where we tried to take turns sleeping. One watching; one sleeping. It was cold and we were both afraid, so we rested and listened and watched.

Perhaps each of us catnapped. We did not speak. I cut spruce boughs for shelter and warmth. We each drew these over us and huddled in the darkness, shivering, the ground so cold its chill seeped through our bodies. We dared not light a fire. We dared not lie down together for warmth, lest we fall asleep and risk the chance of someone creeping up on us in the night and capturing us. Or killing us as we slept.

The antler bone felt odd on my finger. I worried it during the night, sliding it back and forth without taking it off. It was snug without being too tight, and I took pride in my craftmanship. It only needed a little smoothing on the inside and it would be perfect. I wondered if Blue Owl liked her ring and whether she was fiddling with hers as I was with mine.

Many thoughts scrambled through my mind that long cold night. I was glad that I hadn't had to kill either One Dog or Speckled Hawk. I had mixed feelings toward One Dog now that I was away from his eagle eye, his ever-present shadow. Were it not for the killing of my parents, I would probably have been good friends, not only with One Dog, but with all the people of the Arapaho. They had taught me much. I had learned a great deal from One Dog. The Arapaho, I decided that night, were not a bad people. They just lived differently than the whites and they had their own peculiar sense of honor and integrity. They had a different view of life and death. They respected all life, but thought nothing of slaying an enemy and defiling a corpse. They had no reverence for any dead except their own. It was, I thought, a strange balance for such a simple people to keep. Yet, it was a kind of balance, one that I did not have.

I still grieved for my folks. And I anguished over Kate, my only hold on my former life. I felt as if I had been on a strange adventure, an almost dreamlike journey, through several kinds of hell and a few moments, here and there, of almost idyllic existence. I had come to love and respect nature and the bounty of the land, along with its immensity and its unfathomable secrets.

And now I was grown and kind of had a wife. I don't know if I loved Blue Owl, truly loved her, as I would have loved a woman of my own kind. Perhaps I was resisting that kind of love. Yet, I cherished her. She was a gentle and sweet lover under the blanket. She gave me much pleasure in that way. But there was the language barrier between us. I could not deny that. I could speak her language fairly well, but she had little inkling of mine, and that was a wall that separated us on an intellectual level. I seldom, if ever, knew what she was really thinking.

She had surprised me by wanting to run away with me. I gave her credit for that. Yet I knew she would have a difficult time in the white man's world. She would not be accepted, at least not back home in Missouri. Most of the people I knew hated Indians, all Indians, and most had never even seen one. Prejudice was a word I knew, but had seldom heard, and I knew I didn't much understand it. The red man was a hated race in my country. I knew that much. But I had found many similarities between the Arapaho and my own people. They had the same emotions, the same kinds of feelings for one another. They were human, like me. Their skins were different, but their insides were not much different from mine.

Blue Owl and I left that place at dawn. The sun was just below the eastern horizon, and a pale cream was spreading over that part of the sky. Overhead, the stars were growing dimmer against a bowl of light blue as the blackness faded beyond the high, snowcapped peaks. We rode out, working our arms and legs to warm them up, get the blood circulating again. I followed Blue Owl along a narrow game trail that was filled with mule deer tracks heading in both directions. She seemed to know her way, and I was happy to know we were still heading south.

We chewed on dried buffalo meat that was hard for me to swallow. We had no water and my throat soon grew parched. I carried the flintlock across my lap, having checked the lock, making sure the flint was set tight and that there was fresh powder in the pan. I wondered if we were going to stay in the high woods the rest of the way.

We were gradually descending by late afternoon, still keeping to the evergreens above the foothills. We had long

since left the game trail when it headed for a higher eleva-
tion. There was no sign of anyone following us, and I rode
up alongside Blue Owl to talk to her.

"Do you think One Dog is following us?" I asked.

"He is drunk. All of the men are drunk."

"Good. Then we are safe."

"I do not know," she said. "We must take care."

"Do you know how far it is to the two rivers?"

"I do not know."

"One sun?" Two suns?"

"Two suns perhaps."

We spent three suns riding to the confluence of the
Cache la Poudre and the South Platte. We slaked our thirst
in the Platte along the way, riding to it only at night, under
cover of darkness. I wish we had thought to bring a water
skin because I was always thirsty when we were away from
the river.

Blue Owl found a ford on the Platte and we crossed
over. We passed that place where the Poudre emptied into
the larger river, and I noticed there were log cabins near
there. We also passed a number of deserted, dilapidated
houses that seemed to have been abandoned for some time.
It felt like riding through a ghost town, but I knew some of
the cabins were inhabited. We passed them in the night to
the yapping of dogs, but nobody lit a lamp or came outside
to investigate.

The next day, we saw the fort and the houses in the distance. My heart soared, as the Arapaho say, like an eagle.
The fort looked to be a large settlement as we approached,
nestled on the plain below the foothills that rose up to the
west of it. And looming over it were the majestic Rocky
Mountains, gleaming white with snow clear down to the
lower levels.

Blue Owl halted her pony.

"You go to the fort?" she asked.

"Yes."

"I have fear."

"I will protect you, Blue Owl."

"I fear the white eyes."

"You do not need to have fear. I am with you."

She smiled at me. It was a weak smile, but enough of an encouragement that I signed to her that we should go on.

"Do you have the shining metal?" she asked, and I knew she was talking about money.

"No."

"You wait," she said, and rummaged through her pouch. She brought out a smaller pouch that was bulging.

"What do you have?" I asked.

"You take," she said, and handed me a small brown pouch that was closed tight with a leather drawstring that puckered the leather. I loosed the drawstring and looked inside.

The pouch was filled with silver and gold coins, even some paper money.

"Where did you get this?" I asked.

"Blue Owl take. Belong to the woman of Little Blue Lizard."

"Where did she get the shining metal?"

"Little Blue Lizard take from white eyes."

So, Blue Owl had stolen the money pouch, knowing we would need it. She was smarter than I had thought. I felt rich. I slipped the pouch inside my trousers, beneath the sash I wore. I grinned at her.

"Food," I told her. "We go."

"Yes," she said, and smiled more warmly this time.

The city was sprawled around the fort, which was itself a sprawl of buildings. In the center of the fort buildings, an American flag flew, flapping in the late afternoon breeze.

I had no idea where to go, but I knew that the heart of the city would be our best bet to find food and lodging. People stared at us as we rode down the main street. Dogs barked at us. Children ran away from us in fright.

That's when I realized what we must look like to all those white faces. Two hated Indians, one with a rifle, riding into their town. Doors slammed shut and people peered at us from behind draped windows.

We reached what I thought was the center of town, a large square surrounded by buildings that reminded me some of home in Kansas City. But these were newer and made of logs and sandstone and clapboard lumber. The largest of these was Avery House, which I took to be a hotel.

I started riding toward it, when some men came out of one of the buildings, a tavern. One ran a few yards and disappeared into the sheriff's office. One of the men from the tavern grabbed my bridle and the pony stopped. Another took Blue Owl's bridle in hand.

In a few seconds we were surrounded by men, all glaring at us. Some had pistols drawn. Others whispered to each other or muttered under their breath. The man who had my bridle in his hands looked to be flushed with drink. His face was ruddy, his nose shiny.

"Well, well, what do we have here?" he said to the crowd. "A young buck and his squaw just ridin' into town as pretty as you please."

"String 'em up," one man yelled from the back of the crowd.

"Scalp 'em," yelled another.

Fear almost choked me to silence. These men were about to become a mob. And a mob, I knew, was dangerous. Mindless.

"Mister, we mean no harm," I said. "We're just looking for sanctuary."

"This 'un speaks English," the ruddy-faced man said. "But he's a damned Rappyhoe, sure as shit."

I looked around for any sympathetic face among the angry crowd, most of whom, I was sure, had been drinking in the tavern. I saw none.

But just then, some men came out of the sheriff's office and made their way through the crowd. Some were carrying rifles and one of them had a double-barreled shotgun in his hands. The first man, who wore a sheriff's star on his shirt, was the first to reach us. Some of the crowd began to melt back.

"Two redskins, Sheriff," one man yelled from inside the cluster.

"Rufe, what you got there?" the sheriff asked the man holding my horse.

"These two red niggers just come a-ridin' up. They must have run off from some reservation."

The sheriff snatched my bridle from Rufe and turned to the crowd.

"You all go back where you came from. I'll handle this. Now, go on, back to your own business."

There were a lot of aws and disappointed grunts from the crowd, but most of them began to disperse. Rufe stayed, but stepped back a few feet. He wore a Colt pistol on his hip and I think he was looking for an excuse to shoot me with it.

"The buck speaks English," Rufe said.

The sheriff looked up at me. Then he looked at the rifle across my lap.

"Let me see that rifle," the sheriff said.

I handed it to him. It was the worst thing I could have done right then. A half-dozen men drew their pistols and aimed every one of them at me.

"You sonofabitch," the sheriff said as he examined the rifle. He turned to one of his deputies and handed him the rifle.

"Sure enough," the deputy said. "I'd recognize that old flintlock anywheres."

The sheriff's men surged forward. Arms reached out for me and before I could react, I was being dragged off my pony.

Bluc Owl didn't make a sound, but as I was being carried away, I saw them go after her and I saw her eyes flare like some wild creature caught in a trap. I struggled to break free, but the men were too strong. One of them hit me in the head with the butt of his pistol. Hard.

Dancing silver stars filled my brain, and then the darkness took them away and plunged me into a black pit. I lost my senses at the bottom of that well of liquid pitch.

Twenty

My head throbbed with a distant pain that I could not reach in the dream. It was as if my head had a heart attached to the back of it, a heart that was pulsing, beating, aching. None of the dream would make sense once I woke up, but while I was in its throes, it all seemed real.

The heart became a hammer, and a large horse was kicking at the handle, sending shoots of pain through my body. I tried to get on the horse, but it kept sliding away from me until it became a buffalo running away from me, its hooves sounding like the beat of a heavy drum deep inside my head. Then the buffalo walked into a lake and sank, dragging me with it because I was holding onto its tail, a tail that kept getting longer and longer until it shrank, pulling me down into the water. I struggled to breathe, and bright lights danced in my head like a swarm of silver fireflies. The lake disappeared, leaving me on a dark island in the middle of an empty prairie where I heard a voice speaking to me in a strange tongue.

That was when I awoke and saw a silhouetted figure standing behind a wall of bars.

"You awake?" the voice said.

I touched the back of my head, felt a small lump there. The bump was tender to my touch and I winced in pain. It took me several seconds to realize where I was. I was lying down on a cot of some sort. A mattress was underneath me. And the man I saw wasn't standing on the other side of a wall of bars. I was the one who was behind bars. Gingerly, I sat up. My head hurt, and it took me another few seconds to focus my eyes on the man who had spoken to me.

"You're awake," he said.

"Where am I?"

"You're in jail. How come you speak English?"

"I'm a white man."

"You don't look like no white man. Where you from?"

"Missouri. Kansas City." I stood up, and the room spun for a moment. "I've got to pee." I crossed my legs. "Real bad."

"There's a chamber pot under your bunk."

I bent down, pulled out the chamber pot. I think it was made of iron. It was heavy. I peed, with my back turned to the man who was watching me. I tried to clear my head. It dawned on me that I was in jail. Locked up like a prisoner. I had escaped one prison and landed in another. I finished peeing and slid the pot back under the bunk. I walked over to the cell door and pushed on it. It was locked.

"How come you locked me up?" I asked. "I've done nothing."

"You got some explaining to do. Ready to talk?"

"About what?"

"About that rifle we took off you for one thing."

"That old flintlock?"

"Yeah."

"Then, will you let me go?"

"You hold on, boy."

The man walked to a door and left me standing there. I heard voices. I looked through the bars into another cell just opposite me. There was someone in it.

"Blue Owl?" I called.

She moved from the bunk and stood up. She looked small and disheveled.

"My husband," she said, and I know my face flushed with embarrassment.

"Did they hurt you, Blue Owl?"

"They gave me food. I made sleep. I have fear."

"Do not worry. They do not have bad hearts. They will let us go, these white eyes."

I was still talking to Blue Owl in Arapaho when the man returned, another man with him.

"You come on out, boy," he said. "We'll do some talking. That a Rappyhoe you was talking to, that squaw yonder?"

"Yes. Arapaho."

"I can't get over how good this boy talks English," the other man said, putting a large key in the lock. He turned it and the tumbler jangled. The cell door opened. I stepped out and the man who had opened the door looked me square in the eyes.

"You try to run and I'll shoot you dead. Hear?"

I nodded.

I spoke to Blue Owl as the two men led me away, into the next room. I told her that I would return. She never let out a sound and the door closed behind us.

A man, the one who had first spoken to me outside when I was still on my pony, was sitting behind a desk. He waved me to a chair. I walked over and sat down. There were two other men seated in chairs on the other side of the desk, like a very small jury, I thought.

The two men who had taken me from my cell stood behind me. The flintlock lay crossways on the desk of the man facing me.

"I'm Sheriff Frank Hall," the man said. "I understand you speak English. What is your name?"

"Jared Sunnedon."

"Sundown?"

"That's close enough. It's a Finnish name, I think. Or Swedish."

"You don't look like no Swede. Except for those blue eyes you got."

"I don't know what I am. An American, I guess."

"I want to know how you come by this flintlock rifle. Did you murder Pawnee Bob for it?"

"Who's Pawnee Bob?"

"Don't get smart with me, Mr. Sundown." He turned and looked at the two men sitting next to him.

"You're sure about this, Clete? You, Davis?"

"Yes, sir, Sheriff. That's Pawnee Bob's rifle all right," Clete said. He was the first man the sheriff had looked at to answer the question.

"Davis?"

"I'd swear on it. Bob never let that rifle out of his sight. Got it back in Lancaster, Pennsylvania, he did. Kilt many a b'ar with it. Buffler too."

"That's what I thought," Hall said. Then he looked back at me.

"So, how come you to have Pawnee Bob Fritz's rifle, Mr. Sundown?"

"I got it off an Arapaho brave named Speckled Hawk. I stole it from him. I don't know where he got it."

"That would be hard to prove, since we don't know any Rappyhoe named Speckled Hawk. We just got your word for it."

"Well, that's all I have is my word. Look, Sheriff, I was captured by a band of Arapaho. They killed my folks, Sven and Hilda Sunnedon. We were in a wagon train heading for Oregon and the master, a man named Cassius Hogg, shot two Arapaho boys for no good reason. When my pa raised Cain about it, Hogg banished us from the wagon train and left us on our own. He scalped those two boys and put their scalps in my pa's wagon. When the Arapaho came upon us, they found the scalps and thought my pa had killed those boys. They killed my folks right on the spot and kidnapped me and my sister Kate. I come here to Fort Collins looking for her."

The sheriff said nothing. He looked up at the two deputies standing behind me and then at Clete and Davis.

"Whoeeee," the sheriff said. "That's quite a story, Mr. Sundown. I don't know whether to believe it or not."

"You can believe it," I said. My head had cleared and I was getting angry. My noggin still hurt, though, and that lump was still there.

"Jesse, where's that stuff them people brought in a few months ago?"

"Out back in the shed," the man behind me said. "They said they found an abandoned wagon, some white folks turned almost to skeleton."

"Was there any name in that stuff?"

"Yeah, there was some letters and a Bible with writing in it. I think they was folks' names writ down."

"Go see what you can find while I ask this feller a few more questions."

Jesse walked back into the jail. I figured there was a back door to the shed out back.

"My folks had a Bible," I said. "Their names were in it."

"We know this Cassius Hogg," Sheriff Hall said. "Anybody with him on that wagon train?"

"Yes. A man named Truitt. Rudy Truitt. Those two traded for my sister. Some Ota, some Utes, stole her from the Arapaho. I think Hogg sold my sister to a family named Pettigrew. I'm trying to find her."

The sheriff exchanged glances with the other men in the room.

Seconds ticked by and I started to sweat.

"You sit still, son," Hall said. "Freddie, strip off the feller's shirt."

The man standing behind me reached down and grabbed my sleeves. He pulled the buckskin shirt off me as slick as you'd skin a squirrel. I sat there bare-chested. Freddie walked around the chair to look at me, my buckskin shirt still in his hand.

"Not a mark on him," Freddie said.

"Maybe he is white," Clete said. "He ain't got no marks or scars on him."

The sheriff leaned forward over his desk and stared at my chest. I wondered if all the men in the room had gone crazy. Their eyes were as wide as boiled eggs. Clete even came over and put his face up close to my chest.

"You know what a Sun Dance is, Mr. Sundown?" Hall asked.

"I heard of it. Some kind of Indian ceremony."

"It's the devil's work," Clete said.

"What is it?" I asked.

"You really don't know?" Hall seemed to be challenging me, trying to catch me in a lie.

"The Arapahos were going to a place for this Sun Dance," I said, "when they were attacked by some Utes. That's when the Utes took Kate and two young Arapaho girls. One Dog hunted the Utes down and winter came on. They never did go to that Sun Dance."

"Humph," the sheriff snorted. "I don't know, boys. Where in hell is that bastard Cameron? Jim said he'd come over to the office to look this feller over."

"I don't know," Freddie said. "Jim should have been here by now."

"Who's Jim Cameron?" I asked.

"He was a friend of Pawnee Bob's. He saw the buck what scalped Bob and took his rifle and possibles."

"He's an eyewitness to Pawnee Bob's murder, kid," Freddie said. "He can damned sure identify you as one of the Rappyhoes what jumped poor old Bob and done him in."

"Well, I damned sure didn't know any Pawnee Bob and I sure as hell didn't kill him," I said.

"You watch your mouth, sonny," Hall said. "You ain't clear of this yet. Give him back his damned shirt, Freddie."

Freddie handed me my shirt and I slipped it on over my head. Which made my head start hurting again.

I wondered what Jesse was doing out back in the shed there. Nobody spoke. They all just stared at me as if I was already a dead man. Maybe on my way to the gallows. I was sweating a lot by then. The quiet only made me sweat more.

"Maybe he's too young to have done one of them Sun Dances," Clete said. "Might have to be a certain age."

"Might," Hall said.

More silence. Then Freddie stood up straight and looked out the window.

"Here comes old Jim now," he said. "He's got an eagle eye. He'll know right off if you had a hand in killing Pawnee Bob."

They all turned to look at the door. It opened and a man in elk skins strode through the door. He was carrying a flintlock rifle just like the one I had taken, curly maple stock and all. It looked exactly like mine.

He was a big man, with a full snowy beard, and wore a fur hat, beaded leggings, moccasins. His shirt was beaded too, and he wore a necklace of bear claws.

He was the most fearsome white man I had ever seen, and his blue eyes glinted with fire as he stopped right in front of me and looked me square in the eye. He put a hand on the hatchet handle jutting from his belt.

I was sure he was going to split my head wide open right then and there.

I stopped sweating and my skin turned ice cold.

Twenty-one

Time seemed to stand still for me.

Tiny spiders scurried up and down my spine until I almost shivered. The knot on my head began to throb again, just like a beating heart. There wasn't a sound in the room until I let out my breath, not realizing I had been holding it.

"Well, Big Jim," Hall said, after what seemed like a million moments had passed by. "Is this one of the bucks that rubbed out Pawnee Bob?"

Cameron startled me then with what he said. He spoke in irregular Arapaho.

"One Dog has the pizzle of a mouse. He has the heart of a worm. He eats buffalo shit with the dogs. Do you sit at his fire and smoke the pipe with that black coward?"

I didn't know whether to answer the man in English or in Arapaho.

Either way, I felt that my life hung in the balance.

Finally, as Cameron drew air through his nostrils, giving him the sound of a fire-breathing dragon, I replied. In English.

"One Dog murdered my folks, Mr. Cameron. I hate him worse than you do."

"Christ," Cameron said, turning to Hall. "What you got here, Frank? A damned captive white kid?"

"I don't know, Jim. You tell me."

"He ain't one of the ones," Cameron said, and I breathed a sigh of relief.

"Are you sure?"

"It was Speckled Hawk's father what kilt Pawnee Bob. I seen him plain as day. I was outnumbered, so I stayed hid, but I seen the red nigger what put Bob's lamp out. Warn't this boy here. Look at his damned skin. He's black from the sun, but there ain't no red in it." He grabbed one of my braids and yanked it. "You ought to cut these off, sonny, start lookin' like a white man."

"He says he stole Pawnee Bob's rifle off'n Speckled Hawk," the sheriff said. "Reckon we ought to believe him?"

"That's up to you, Frank. He ain't no redskin and he didn't rub out Pawnee Bob."

I heard a clumping sound from the jail and a moment later, Jesse entered the room. He was carrying some items in his arms that I recognized.

"What you got there, Jesse?" Hall asked.

Jesse dumped the items on Hall's desk.

"They's a Bible here, all right. Some letters and stuff. Bible has the name Sunnedon in it."

"That's my ma's Bible," I said. "I recognize it."

The sheriff picked up the Bible, flapped the cover open, read the inscription on the flyleaf.

"What'd you say your ma's name was, Mr. Sundown?" he asked.

"Hilda. Hilda Sunnedon," I said.

"That's what it says here. Got your pa's name here, yours and your sister's, I reckon."

"That's our family Bible."

I was desperate to convince the sheriff that I was who I said I was. I got the feeling that he didn't want to believe me, no matter what proof I had.

"Well, I got things to do, Frank," Cameron said. Then he looked at me. "You aim to keep that rifle?"

"I do."

"Well, you come by it honest, I reckon. I got its mate right here. Both made by the same gunsmith back in Lancaster, Pennsylvania. It shoots true, you know how to use it."

I didn't say anything.

"It's stolen goods," Clete said.

"Shut up, Wilson," Hall said.

So, now I knew Clete Wilson's full name.

"Jim, he's got him a squaw. She's back in the jail."

"Oh?" Jim's eyebrows arched like a pair of inchworms.

"Want to talk to her?" Hall said.

"What for?"

"I don't know. She don't speak no English."

"You leave Blue Owl alone," I said.

The sheriff reared back in his chair and looked at me as if I had just soiled his entire office.

"Well, now," Hall said, "that ain't no call for you to get sassy, Mr. Sundown. Clete, bring the squaw out. Maybe we can clear up this mess once and for all."

I glared at the sheriff. I blamed him for the terrible throbbing in my skull. I was hungry and tired and scared half out of my wits. The people in that room were not friendly, and now they wanted to drag Blue Owl into my troubled life and make us both victims of their suspicions and downright prejudice.

"Clothes make the man," my mother used to say, and now I knew what she meant. Because I looked like an Indian, all of these white men took me for one. I was the lowliest of the low in their eyes. And even if by now everybody knew I was as American as they were, as white as they were, and my name was Jared Sunnedon, I was dressed like an Arapaho, with braided hair and dark skin. Therefore, I was still an outsider, a pariah, an outcast from my own tribe.

I kept my mouth shut. I heard a commotion in the jail. A few seconds later, Clete wrestled Blue Owl into the room. She was fighting against being manhandled and Clete had his hands full.

"You don't have to hurt her," I said to Clete. "She's just not used to white folks."

Clete released her. She saw me and ran over to stand beside me. Her lips were quivering, but she didn't cry. In fact, she didn't let out a sound.

Cameron looked at her, rubbed his chin.

"Well?" Hall said. "What do you make of the squaw, Jim?"

"I don't know," Cameron said. "She looks like a damned Rappyhoe, but they's somethin' different about her."

"What do you mean?" Hall asked.

Cameron didn't answer the sheriff. Instead, he spoke to Blue Owl in Arapaho. He didn't speak it very well, more like a man speaking pidgin English, but I got his meaning.

"You girl," he said, "you people squaw?"

"I am Tsis-tis-tas," she said.

I had no idea what Blue Owl meant. I had never heard those words before.

"She ain't no Arapaho," Cameron said. "She says she's Cheyenne."

"Cheyenne?" Hall said.

I turned to look at Blue Owl, as dumbfounded as they were.

"You tell story, girl," Cameron said. "You no One Dog woman?"

"I am Tsis-tis-tas. One Dog steal me when I had ten summers. I am prisoner like Sundown." She made the sign of the setting sun.

"Looks like you got yourself a pair of runaways, Frank," Cameron said. "This squaw was captured by One Dog and his band when she was ten years old. She ain't no Rappyhoe."

"Well, I'll be damned," Hall said. Then he looked at me. "This your squaw, Mr. Sundown? I noticed you two got horn rings on your fingers, like you two was married."

"In her eyes maybe," I said. "She might think I'm her husband. She helped me escape from One Dog's camp."

The men in the room all cleared their throats. I could almost see their evil minds working. Clete and Davis both wore looks of disgust on their faces.

"Well," Hall said, "I don't reckon these two committed any crimes. Leastways, not here in Fort Collins. I reckon I'll let 'em go their own ways. But there's another matter I got to take up with you, Mr. Sundown. Jared."

"Yes?"

"I know this Hogg and his partner, Truitt. You'd best stay clear of them two. They're bad medicine. I don't have enough evidence to arrest them, but I keep my eye on them when they're in town. They come and they go and I suspicion they're up to no good. Both of 'em been jailed for fighting and drunkenness.

"And that family you mentioned, the ones who you say have your sister with them, Pettigrew."

"Yes?" I said, leaning forward in my chair.

"They're a bunch of no-accounts, and left town a day or so ago. Headed north, I heard, owing money all over town."

"Do you know where they were going?"

Hall shook his head. "I don't know and I don't care. Good riddance. That Amos Pettigrew is one mean sonofabitch from what I've heard. I wouldn't put it past him to buy your sister from a bastard like Hogg, if that's what he did."

"I'll be looking for her," I said. "If you let us go."

"Well, I guess that might settle it. I took a pouch of money off you. Where'd you get it?"

My heart sank. I didn't know where the money Blue Owl gave me came from, but if I told the truth they might keep her in jail. It was probably stolen off white people that the Arapaho killed.

"It's money my pa gave me," I said. "I hid it from One Dog. He never knew I had it."

"Well, you keep the rifle and I'll give you back your money and those ponies we've got in the livery. You and the squaw can go on your way. No hard feelings?"

"No hard feelings." I stood up. I looked down at Blue Owl and smiled.

"We are free," I told her.

"We'll give you an escort out of town, Mr. Sundown," Hall said. "Just in case the white folks here still think you're a redskin. But if I were you, I'd take Jim Cameron's advice and get rid of them pigtails."

"Yes, sir," I said. "I'd like my knife back too, and our pouches and such."

Hall smiled and got up from his desk.

"You'll get back everything we took offen you, Jared. You just stay out of trouble, hear?"

"Yes, sir, I will."

A half hour later, Blue Owl and I were on our ponies. The sheriff and his two deputies flanked us as we rode through town. At the northern edge, he reined up.

"That road there is the Cherokee Trail," he said. "If the Pettigrews were going anywhere, they'd probably head north. I wish you good luck, Jared. What's your squaw's name anyway?"

"She's not my squaw. But her name is Blue Owl."

"Well, this is as far as we go. You two are on your own."

"Thank you, Sheriff Hall. I'm much obliged."

"I'm sorry about your folks. I think somebody buried them. I put that Bible in your kit, case you wanted it as a memento."

Blue Owl and I rode north to the two rivers. I looked around for the pile of stones and found it, well off the trail.

"What you do?" she asked.

"I look for something."

She held my pony's reins while I slid off him and walked over to the pile of stones. I pushed them away and saw the hole in the ground. I smiled. Ormly House had left me a large powder flask, which was full, and a pouch full of lead balls. I held them up and showed them to Blue Owl.

"For my rifle."

She smiled.

We drank at the river and rode on.

"Where we go?" she asked.

"I look for my sister."

"Blue Owl go where you go, Sundown."

I got back on my pony, put the powder and ball in the pouch slung over my shoulder. It was getting right heavy.

That night when we stopped, well off the trail, I brought out the Bible that had belonged to my parents. Memories of them flooded through me as I held it in my hands.

This was all that I had of them, but it was enough. When I found Kate, my life would be full and complete.

That night, I cut off my braids.

Twenty-two

From where we camped that night, I could see the lights of La Porte. They winked on, one by one, and I realized that the settlement was larger than I had thought when we rode through it the night before. When we hunted the elk, we had been higher up and I hadn't realized there was a settlement there.

"Why you look?" Blue Owl asked.

"There are people down there."

"Yes. White eyes. They make trade."

A trading post? I hadn't known.

"How do you know this?" I asked.

"One Dog trade there."

As I watched, I saw riders come into the little village that lay on a hill across from the junction of the two rivers. Men from Fort Collins, I supposed.

When the wind was right, I could hear laughter and the tink of a piano. It made me very homesick, and very lonely. I knew then that I longed for companionship, the company of people I could converse with in my own language. There was a longing in me to go down there and perhaps buy a beer, join in the singing.

"Why you cut hair?" Blue Owl asked.

"I am no longer one of the people."

"Blue Owl cut hair."

"No," I said. "Your hair pretty."

"I cut hair," she said, and pulled my knife from its sheath and ran off.

"You bad girl," I called to her.

She giggled in the darkness, and I turned back to my fascination with the activities around the little village of La Porte.

It was odd, I thought, how quickly human beings can adapt to an environment. When I was with the Arapaho, I lived that life and developed habits that allowed me to adapt to their ways. Now, I longed for a different life and I suppose memory played a part, because when I looked at the little cabins and the trading post, a longing arose up in me to walk down there and announce that I had returned to my own kind after being lost in the wilderness.

But I knew better than to do anything like that. I was still a stray cat, half wild, not yet ready to fully accept the white man's civilization. I had had a taste of it in Fort Collins, and when I looked back on that recent experience, I realized how it could have turned out differently if I had not been able to prove my identity. Clothes did make the man. And a whole lot else. Yes, I could be shorn of my Indian braids, but my garb shouted Indian, wild man, untamed outcast.

What kept me fascinated for so long was that I knew Kate was somewhere nearby. Perhaps not in La Porte, but somewhere near there. Were some of the Pettigrews down there at that very moment, drinking ale, or whiskey, or wine? Was Amos Pettigrew sitting at a table with his friends bragging about the bond servant in his household? I was almost desperate to know exactly where Amos Pettigrew was at that moment, and consequently, where my sister was on this chill spring night.

There was a deep sadness in my heart as I gazed down at La Porte. I thought of Kansas City and how different it was from a small frontier settlement like this one. My feelings were all mixed up. I wanted something that was just out of my reach. And I really didn't know what it was just then.

Blue Owl returned, slid my knife back in its scabbard. She sat down next to me and I strained to see what she had done to her hair.

"You like?" she said, patting her shortened hair.

"You look like a boy."

She giggled.

"Am I not pretty to you?"

"Yes. You are pretty. But you are scalped."

She laughed, and the sound of her laughter made me realize what a special person she was. I don't know if I loved her or not, but I was grateful to her. She had made my nights with the Arapaho pleasurable, and had helped me escape without thought of her own safety. She had risked her life for me, and there was no higher calling in life. I put my arm around her waist, and she snuggled up close to me.

"Look," she said a few minutes later. "To the river."

Riders streamed away from the South Platte, heading toward the trading post. Their silhouettes were dim and hard to see, but there was something about the way they rode and what they rode.

Spotted ponies.

I felt Blue Owl's body stiffen.

"Who are they?" I asked.

"Ota," she breathed.

"Ota?"

"Yes. They go to buy the firewater."

The hairs on the back of my head prickled my skin.

On the ride out of town with Sheriff Hall and his men, we had spoken some about the Pettigrews and now I remembered that conversation.

"Is this Amos Pettigrew a farmer?" I had asked.

"He claims to be a farmer."

"What does that mean?"

"Let's just say that I've heard that Pettigrew is an enterprising man. He buys and sells goods over to La Porte. He and his boys get a lot of packages from the stage that comes here once or twice a month from Santa Fe."

"What kind of goods?" I had asked.

The sheriff shrugged. "We don't pry into people's lives much, Mr. Sundown."

"Does he sell things to the Indians around here?"

"Not that I know of. It's illegal to sell whiskey or guns to the Indians. I don't know for sure what was in those packages besides grain. Could be he buys grain for his stock. The man keeps pretty much to himself."

"Seems to me you don't like Amos Pettigrew much."

"I don't know the man that well."

"Well, you don't think much of him," I said.

"I don't think of him much at all."

I thought of that conversation now and wondered if I had missed anything.

Amos Pettigrew claimed to be a farmer, yet he was buying and selling merchandise he had shipped to him from Santa Fe. What could that be? Guns? Whiskey?

I turned back to Blue Owl.

"Did One Dog ever buy firewater from the trader here?"

"I do not know," she said.

I thought again of what Sheriff Hall and said. "Grain." With sour mash, Pettigrew could make whiskey, sell it to the Utes. Would he also sell them guns?

"I will go to the town of the white eyes tomorrow," I said to her.

"Why?"

"I look for my sister."

"She is there?"

"She is somewhere near that town of the white eyes."

"You know this?"

"I know this. Let us sleep now, Blue Owl. I will watch. You sleep."

"Yes. I will sleep," she said.

Tomorrow I would buy us blankets and canteens, maybe a tent, some staples, cooking utensils. La Porte was a trading post. I would go alone and take Blue Owl's pony to carry the goods I would buy. We had eaten the dried buffalo meat, and she had some roots that served as vegetables, but were very dry and hard to chew. She had not eaten much and neither had I. We were both still shaken over our experience in Fort Collins. I looked at her and thought how brave she was, how sweet she looked in sleep.

Sometime after Blue Owl had fallen asleep, I saw the Utes leave the trading post and cross the river. Like wraiths, they disappeared in the night. Finally, the lights of the town began to wink out and the music stopped. The tavern, or wherever the voices and music were coming from, put out its lamps as well, and I was alone in the quiet. Blue Owl slept straight through. I didn't have the heart to awaken her and take to the ground myself. I dozed and walked around to keep warm, wishing I had a fire, but knowing that Utes were around and would smell the smoke, seek us out.

Blue Owl awoke before dawn.

She went off in the bushes and then returned.

"You do not awaken Blue Owl," she said.

"I did not have a wish to sleep."

"You tired."

"I go to buy blankets and cooking pots, food to eat."

"Where?"

"Down there." I pointed to what I thought was the trading post among the small buildings on the slope above the Cherokee Trail.

"Blue Owl go with you?"

"No. I will take your pony to carry what I buy with the shining metal."

"Buy hatchet," she said.

"Yes."

I rode down to La Porte, but took a long way around so that I would not be seen coming from where we were camped. I rode some distance north until I could no longer see any of the buildings, then descended onto the Cherokee Trail. The sun was halfway up the sky to its zenith when I saw the sign: CHEROKEE TRAIL TRADING POST. Underneath it: BILL JENKINS, PROP. I rode toward the log building. I tied the ponies to the hitch rail out front, carried my rifle with me, and walked onto the porch and into the store, which was open for business.

There were half a dozen horses already tied up at the hitch rail so I knew there would be people inside. I wasn't prepared for the two I saw, sitting at a table in one part of the room. They had a pail of beer and two glasses and hardly looked up when I entered. But they did look up for a minute and I saw their faces.

There, not twenty feet away, sat Cassius Hogg and Rudy Truitt.

They had not recognized me.

I walked to the counter. The other men in the place were playing cards at tables. There was a strong smell of beer and cider in the room, along with the other odors.

"I want to buy some things," I said.

"We don't sell to Injuns in the daytime," the man said.

"I'm not an Indian. I'm a white man."

He cocked his head and looked at me closely.

"Well, you speak the lingo good enough, but you don't look much white to me."

"I will buy clothes too." I took out my money pouch and reached in, put some twenty-dollar gold pieces on the counter.

"Well, yes, sir, then. Money talks, eh? I'm Bill Jenkins. Where you from?"

I didn't know what to say. I remembered Ormly House saying that he had come down from Fort Laramie. Perhaps he had stopped in here.

"Fort Laramie. I'm trying to find my friend, Ormly House."

"Ormly came through here a few days ago. You just missed him. Now, let's get you some clothes and whatnot. You just tell me what you want and I'll bring them."

"I'll need a pannier and some rope to carry what I buy on my packhorse." I didn't say "pony" because I knew that would make him suspicious all over again.

I gave Jenkins a list of what I wanted to buy, wondering if I had enough money for all of it. But I had counted the paper, silver, and gold and it had come to over one hundred dollars. While he was counting it all up, I fitted the wooden pannier to the back of Blue Owl's pony, and tied it on with diamond hitches like my father had once shown me.

When I was almost all packed, I heard a voice.

"You there. Turn around."

I turned around and there on the porch stood Hogg and Truitt. They both wore sidearms. Colts, I think.

"Do I know you?" Hogg asked.

My blood froze.

He had his right hand resting on the butt of his pistol.

And my rifle was inside, leaning against the counter.

My answer, I thought, might well decide my fate. If I said the wrong thing, I could be dead within a very short time. If I didn't, I might just get to live.

But, for that long precarious moment, I was tongue-tied, and shaking like a leaf inside my buckskins.

Twenty-three

Here he was, I thought. A man I hated so much I wanted to strangle him with my bare hands. But he was armed and I was not.

Cassius Hogg was bracing me, ready to draw his pistol and shoot me dead if I told him the truth, if I told him who I really was.

I thought of a boy back home I knew, back in Kansas City. He was younger than I, and kind of a dolt. His parents were not gifted much with brains either, and it was unlikely a man like Hogg would have ever heard of any of them.

"My name's Nickerson," I said, pitching my voice a lot lower than it usually was, "Andy Nickerson. Out of Fort Laramie. Been up in the Medicine Bows hunting elk. Lost my traps in a flood, stole me a couple of Rappyhoe ponies, and am headin' out for Santa Fe."

Where I got all that, I don't know. Maybe there's just one big mind in the whole universe and it's God's great mind and we just dip into it when we need to and find all kinds of useful thoughts.

"Well, you looked kinda familiar," Hogg said. "But I reckon we ain't never met."

"Not likely."

"It ain't him," Truitt said, his tongue thick with drink.

I didn't say anything, believing that the less I said, the better.

"My mistake," Hogg said. "I'm Cassius Hogg and this here's Rudy Truitt. Buy you a drink?"

"Naw, I got to get to Fort Collins. Hope to meet up with my pard."

"Who would that be?" Hogg said. "Might be I know the man."

"Ormly. Ormly House."

Hogg and Truitt exchanged glances.

"Yeah, he come through here a while back. Seems like he was from Fort Laramie too."

I pulled the rope tight on the pannier and stood there, hoping the two men would go on back inside and drink another pail of warm beer.

"Well, thanks," I said.

The two men went back inside the trading post. I heaved a sigh and waited a few minutes, then walked in to retrieve my rifle.

"Anything else?" Jenkins asked when I picked up my rifle.

I looked around, then shook my head.

"You're all settled up then."

"Sir, would you mind walking outside with me? I want to talk to you in private."

"Why, sure. I reckon I can do that. Ain't nobody in here goin' to steal nothin'."

He laughed and followed me out of the store.

"What was it you wanted to say, young feller?"

"I'm wondering about a family in these parts, sir. Name of Pettigrew. Amos Pettigrew in particular. Do you have an acquaintance with this man?"

The expression on Jenkins's face changed markedly, freezing up in a suspicious scowl.

"How come you be askin' about Amos Pettigrew?"

"A friend in Fort Laramie asked me to pass on his regards."

"Oh, well, that's different, I guess. Yeah, I know Amos pretty well. Do some business with him."

"Can you give me directions to his farm? I'd like to stop by and relieve myself of the obligation I'm under."

"Well, yeah, he's got him a farm yonder, over the hill. But he ain't there."

"Oh. He left?"

Jenkins chuckled.

"Up the canyon," he said, pointing across the river. "He goes up there to trade every spring. It's quite a ride. You may not want to take the time."

"No, maybe not. Well, thanks, Mr. Jenkins."

"You have yourself a safe journey to Santy Fe, young feller."

I untied the ponies and climbed up on the back of the one I was riding. I saluted Jenkins as he stood on the porch, laid my rifle across my lap, and rode away. I felt the stares on my back and knew I had better head for Fort Collins until I was well out of sight, then double back to where Blue Owl was waiting for me.

I found a ford, a small one, barely accessible, farther down the South Platte and crossed over. I knew I'd have to cross the Poudre too, and rode into the foothills. I knew I could cross at that wide bend where we hunted the elk. It would be a long ride, but I had some hardtack and jerky to gnaw on, plus a couple of canteens that I could fill from the Poudre.

It was late afternoon when I got back to our camp. I had gotten lost a couple of times and had to ride close to the Cherokee Trail to get my bearings. I don't know if anyone from the trading post saw me, but I hoped not.

Blue Owl was happy to see me and she helped me unload the bulging pannier. When she laid out the things that I had bought, she picked up each. I bought her a little mirror and some candy, which she had never tasted before. She beamed as she chewed on a licorice stick and examined the small kettle, the cups, and a cook pot. She gazed at herself in the mirror and made faces, smiling all the time.

We made love that night under the lean-to I had put up from canvas I had bought. She delighted in cutting the stakes with the new hatchet. We did not make a fire that night, but I told her I would make one in the morning and would cook for her. There was no word in Arapaho for "breakfast," but she knew what "morning food" was. I was content. I did not tell her that we were going to ride up the Cache la Poudre to look for my sister. I would do that after I had cooked her some eggs and bacon and her belly was full. I had bought a coffeepot and some Arbuckle's coffee too, which was my surprise for her. She asked me over and over what was in the sack, but I wouldn't tell her.

Blue Owl would never have that breakfast. And I never got to light a fire the next morning. She heard them coming long before I did, and told me that we must hide.

"Somebody come," she said. "You, me, we hide."

"Where?"

"From the town of the white eyes."

She pointed down toward La Porte.

I put fresh powder in the pan of my rifle, blew away the excess, and we waited. I heard horses coming up through the trees. Then, it was quiet for a long time.

"Maybe they went away," I whispered.

She put her ear to the ground. It grew very quiet. I waited. She lifted her head and looked at me.

"Gone?" I asked.

"I do not know."

"Maybe just some hunters," I said in English to myself.

We got up and walked back to the lean-to. Nothing had been disturbed and there were no signs that anyone had ridden up on horseback. I laid my rifle against a small pine tree within easy reach and started to chop kindling with the hatchet.

"I know who you are, you sonofabitch."

The voice boomed and I must have jumped a half foot. I dropped the hatchet and stretched to grab my rifle.

I recognized the voice.

It was Hogg, but I couldn't see him.

He and Truitt stepped out from a clump of trees. Blue Owl ran up, bent down, and snatched up the hatchet.

"Got yourself a squaw, eh, Jared? Well, you drop that rifle, sonny."

Both Hogg and Truitt had rifles in their hands.

"Leave us alone, Hogg," I said.

He lifted his rifle to his shoulder. He was no more than forty yards away.

But Truitt shot first. The crack of the Winchester sounded like a bullwhip.

I brought my rifle up and took aim an instant after Truitt fired. I put the blade front sight on his chest, lined it up with the rear buckhorn, pulled the set trigger, then fired.

A cloud of white smoke billowed from the muzzle of my rifle. Orange flame squirted from the barrel in a shower of sparks. I could not see through the thick white smoke.

I heard a cry from nearby, and turned to see Blue Owl crumpling to her knees. A crimson stain blossomed like a flower on her chest.

I drew my knife and ran through the smoke, straight toward Hogg and Truitt.

Hogg fired his rifle, but the bullet whistled past me. I saw Truitt lying on the ground, blood gushing from his chest.

Hogg was working the lever to jack in another cartridge when I hit him in the gut with my head, bowling him over backward. I slapped at his rifle and it tumbled from his grasp. His whiskey breath assaulted my nostrils.

"You bastard," Hogg growled, the breath knocked out of him.

I got to my knees and jabbed my knife at him. Hogg crabbed around and stood up. He drew his Colt pistol, but I hit him before the weapon cleared his holster. I sailed a roundhouse left to his face, struck him high, near the temple. He kicked me hard in the shin and pain shot through my leg.

Then he brought his pistol up. He started to bring it level with my head. He cocked it, and the metallic sound sent shivers up my spine. I dove at him, brandishing my knife, slashing at his torso.

The knife blade sliced through his shirt and drew blood. I ducked, just as he squeezed the trigger of his Colt. The explosion deafened me, as I windmilled my arms trying to bring him down, to put the knife to his throat.

Hogg fought me off with his left hand. He was heavier than I was, and very strong. A fist hammered me in the side, knocking wind from my lungs. I whirled and jabbed at him with the knife. He swung the pistol around, and was thumbing back on the hammer when I struck his arm.

He cried out in pain as the knife cut him just above his wrist. The pistol fell from his grasp and he dove for it, cursing and bleeding from his wrist like a stuck pig.

My fury was more than a match for his bulk and strength. I waded into him just as his fingers touched the butt of his pistol. I drove the knife hard into his side and gave it a twist. I felt rib bone and gristle, and blood gushed out before I could completely withdraw the blade. I struck him again in the arm, and then, as he weakened and started to roll over on his back, I plunged the knife into his stomach, once, twice, a third time. Hard and fast. The smell of his bowels wafted up to my nostrils and he groaned in pain.

"You got me, Sunnedon," he rasped. "Damn you."

"You're the one who is damned, Hogg. I hope you rot in hell for what you did to my folks."

"I . . . I . . ." he started to say, but then his body convulsed and his eyes flapped closed.

I heard a click behind me and turned.

Truitt was sitting up, blood all over his chest, and aiming his Colt at me.

I threw myself flat down and grabbed Hogg's cocked pistol. I swung it around to bear on Truitt.

He was too slow and I fired point-blank. The bullet slammed into him and knocked him back down. The lead tore off part of his nose and blew out most of his brains, the back of his skull flying through the air like a pie plate.

Breathless, I stood up. Hogg was dead. I walked over to Truitt, cocking the pistol in case I had to shoot him again. I looked down into his dead, staring eyes that were turning to frost. I could still hear the echoes of the gunshots and see the afterimage of bright orange flame glowing in my eyes.

I started to shake as I walked back to where Blue Owl lay on the ground, sprawled there like a broken doll.

She let out a small gasp as I knelt down beside her. There was so much blood on her chest, I winced at the sight.

She tried to speak, but no sound would come out. I drew her into my arms and held her bloody body tight against my own. I felt a small quiver as she shuddered with her last breath. I looked down at her innocent face. Her eyes were closed and she was still.

It was at that moment that I realized I loved Blue Owl.

I truly loved her.

And now, she was gone.

Forever.

Twenty-four

I made a scaffold for Blue Owl and set it on a ridge that faced the rising sun. There were lots of spruce and pine trees around it, and I set it in front of a large juniper that would keep the mountain winds from blowing her bones away. I bathed her and made her as pretty as I could. I missed her when I put her atop the structure, and I've missed her every day since.

I took the two Winchesters and the Colt pistols that had belonged to Hogg and Truitt. I cleaned out what money they had and put it with the rest of the money in my pouch. I took the best horse they had, a young, strong sorrel gelding, with its saddle and bags, and made it my own. I tied their bodies to the two pinto ponies, and rode down to the trading post.

"Mr. Jenkins, I'm going to leave the bodies of two men outside your store here," I said. "Cassius Hogg and Rudy Truitt. They jumped me and my woman and I killed them both. In self-defense. If you've got a sheriff here, you tell him. If Sheriff Frank Hall is who you go to, then you tell him what I told you."

"Lord God Almighty, you done what?"

"You heard me. Now, I'm going after Amos Pettigrew, up the Poudre, and if anybody follows me, I'll kill them, sure as I'm standing here. You got that?"

"Well, yes, but Good God Almighty, son. You got any witnesses?"

"They killed my witness and I killed them. I'm a dangerous man, Jenkins, from here on out. Now you know all you need to know. And I want to buy something before I set out."

"Well, yes, sir, what is it? Anything I got."

"I want about a half-dozen writing tablets and a dozen lead pencils. You got 'em?"

"I do, I do."

Poor Mr. Jenkins. He didn't know what to make of what I told him. But he walked out with me and saw the bodies, stiff as boards by then, draped over two Indian ponies. I thought he was going to gag on his own breath

"Say, what's your name?" he called after me as I rode away.

"Just call me Sundown."

I was dressed in new clothes and I had on Truitt's hat. It was the better fit of the two I had to choose from. I didn't look in the mirror, but I bet I didn't look like a damned Arapaho anymore. I rode back up to where Blue Owl and I had camped, put the pannier on the other horse, a dappled gray mare, Truitt's, and packed my few belongings. I slung one of the pistols from the saddle horn and carried the spare Winchester and my flintlock on the packhorse. I had plenty of cartridges and put one Winchester in its scabbard. I left the extra saddle and other items hidden under a blue spruce, and covered everything with cut boughs.

Then I rode toward Cache la Poudre Canyon, following the sun.

It was rugged going through rough, unknown country. There were lots of rocks and trees, steep slopes, and I knew the hills rose high above the Poudre. But I wanted to be well away from the confluence of the two rivers, La Porte, and the wagon road up the canyon. I had no idea how far up the Poudre Amos Pettigrew had gone, but I figured that I would catch sight of his camp eventually. I knew I would have to find a place where I could descend to the road and not be seen. Then I would decide whether to go up or down. And most probably, I would have to cross the river and travel through the woods on the other side.

I did not find the river or the road that first day, so I made camp under a rocky outcropping, thick with trees, so that I had protection on three sides. I knew I was in the land of the Utes, and I knew how dangerous they were. So I made no fire, and I did not unsaddle my horse or take the pannier off the packhorse. I loosened cinches and ropes and hobbled both animals, and kept them on lead ropes just in case something spooked them and they broke their hobbles.

The air was clean and fresh and thin at that altitude, and I felt invigorated as I set up my camp for the night. Being up there, so high and away from civilization, gave me a chance to collect my thoughts, reflect on all that had happened in the past few days, and adapt to my new surroundings. I missed Blue Owl and I wished she could have been up there with me as I gazed at all the green and the clear blue sky, with the high, snowcapped peaks at my back and shadows stretching long down the foothills.

I listened long and hard for any sounds, but heard nothing. No voices, no hoofbeats. Just a deep silence up there under the outcropping. I could see then why some men took to the mountains and never wanted to leave. There was such peace up there, in that place, and it seeped into me as the night slowly stole away the day and the darkness flowed into the hills and trees. Even the horses were quiet at that solemn hour just after dusk, and I was grateful for the silence, the deep hush that seemed to settle in the trees and surround me.

I slept, my rifle and pistol by my side, both within easy reach, and only awoke once, to relieve myself. Then, back into the arms of Morpheus, until dawn's rosy fingers touched my face and I opened my eyes to see the sun's rays simmering just below the eastern horizon. I was eating jerky and hardtack as the sun came up, tightening the cinches on the saddle, and taking up the slack in the pannier rope. There had been some grain in one of the saddlebags, and I gave each horse half a hatful. Then I rode through the morning, careful to avoid low limbs that might strike the pack and loosen it, climbing ever higher until I was in the rugged mountains, the foothills far below me.

I angled ever southward, toward the Poudre, and finally came to the large canyon where I could hear the river's muffled roar. The sun was melting some of the snow higher up, and I knew the river was probably raging with spring runoff.

I tied up the horses and walked to a small promontory that jutted out over the gorge. I gazed downward and saw the Poudre, foaming as it raced through twists and turns marked by large boulders. I don't think I've ever seen a more beautiful sight than that river shooting down a steep passage marked by many small bends. It seemed like a living thing. The sun filled its spray with tiny rainbows, and the sound it made was the sound of raw energy, unfettered power. That river was a mighty thing, unlike the slow-moving Platte or the Missouri or even the Mississippi. I stood there, high above it, and grew giddy just watching it run.

I looked up the gorge to see if there was a place where I might ride down. I could see the wagon road, just barely, from where I stood. I saw no place, but figured there might be a ravine or small canyon just beyond the next rise. On the other side, I saw many such places and water streamed from all of them, emptying into the Poudre.

I walked back to where I had tied the horses and climbed into the saddle. I stayed close to the line I had marked in my mind as being the river, and climbed still another ridge. As I rode, I began to wonder if I would find a place on this side where I could descend to the river. The mountains seemed to be getting steeper and the horses were feeling the strain of all that climbing.

But I did find a place, and almost missed it.

There was such a jumble of ridges and shallow valleys up there and the going was so rough, I lost track of the map in my mind. We rode around huge deadfalls and massive boulders and after a while, everything began to look the same. But I topped a small ridge and looked down into a deep gully choked with brush, lined with scrub pines and stunted spruce, elk-ravaged junipers. Then I saw a lot of elk and deer tracks heading down that way, and I figured that this was where they walked to get down to the river where they could drink at night.

And when I got to the bottom of the gorge, or near the bottom, I found a game trail. I turned onto it and headed south. Soon, I heard the soft roar of the Poudre and moments later, I emerged at a wide place where I could see the road and the river.

I waited and looked both ways, like a man at a city

crossroads heavy with wagon traffic. The road was on my side of the river for a ways, then crossed to the other side at a long flat stretch of the river. A ford. The water looked shallow enough even with the river running as full as it was. I realized that I was in a huge flat valley, wedged in between the towering mountains and the lower ranges above the foothills. There were game tracks everywhere.

I rode to the ford and crossed the river. I was going to ride the road, but thought better of it. For a time, I knew I could stay to the trees, keep the road in sight, and not be seen. I saw heavy wagon ruts on the road, and knew that I must be well below the place where Pettigrew had gone.

My decision turned out to be the correct one. After leaving the valley, I stayed to the rugged woods, climbing up and down small hillocks, fighting my way through treacherous footing. A little later I saw the smoke, just a wisp at first, then a gray pall spread out like a blanket over the river. There, just beyond a bend in the river, there was another wide place on both sides. On my side of the river, I saw a cabin with its chimney spewing smoke into the air. The breeze took it and spread it out.

My heart started pumping fast.

The packhorse whickered, and I whirled to look at it as I jumped inside my skin. Sweat oozed from my palms.

I rode well away from the river, up a shallow draw, and tied the horses to some brush. I grabbed the Winchester and walked atop the ridge and then down a slope, creeping along like a stalking hunter. My nerves were raw and my stomach tied up in knots. I crept to a place where I had a full view of the cabin.

I went closer, until I could hear voices, male and female.

Someone inside was arguing or yelling, and I tried to separate the voices, isolate them to any memory I had. I did not hear Kate's voice. I crept closer, and then my heart seemed to stop dead still.

Across the river, on the other side from where the cabin stood, there was a shelf well above it and I saw the cones of Indian teepees through the trees.

Those had to be Utes there, I thought.

And then, as if to prove my suspicion, I saw ponies with riders pouring from the camp and riding down to the river. Two men came out of the cabin and waved to the Utes, who crossed the river. I counted a dozen braves.

The two men went to one of the wagons and opened the tailboard. They pulled out some boards and laid them flat on the ground, then began stacking goods atop the boards.

There were cooking pots, blankets, rifles and pistols, hats, and all sorts of trade goods.

Evidently, I had come just in time to see the Pettigrews lay out their trade goods. The Utes must have just made their camp there, and were coming for a look before they traded for anything. Because the braves were not leading packhorses laden with whatever Pettigrew wanted.

I scanned the ridge where the teepees stood. I didn't see any women or children. Only men, a line of them looking down at the cabin, watching to see what happened.

And then I saw her. Kate. She came out of the cabin and walked well away from the men and the wagons, toward the river. She was carrying two wooden buckets yoked across her back. I had to stare hard to be sure, but it was Kate.

She knelt by the river and dipped a bucket into it.

She was four hundred yards away. So close.

I swallowed hard, and then I had to close my eyes to stop the seep of tears.

I had found my sister, all right, but she was still out of reach.

I watched her walk back, lugging the heavy pails of water. I wanted to call out to her, tell her that I was there.

But I knew better.

I had to find a way to take her away from Pettigrew and not get killed accomplishing that difficult task.

Twenty-five

Some of the Utes went to the whiskey and started making sign. I picked up the gabble of their conversation, but could not understand a word. The older man started pushing them away. The younger man walked over to help him. The older man, whom I took to be Amos Pettigrew, gestured that he would not sell them whiskey. He started yelling at them.

"Tomorrow. After trade. After trade."

The Utes backed away, but made obscene gestures at Pettigrew.

The younger man pointed to the other goods and tried to lead the Utes toward the blankets and cooking utensils. The Utes signed no and went to the rifles and pistols. They began picking them up, playing with them. Only, they weren't playing. They wanted guns and whiskey. Again, Pettigrew yelled at them and made sign that he would not sell the guns to them.

"Tomorrow. You bring gold. No guns. No whiskey. Not now."

Gold? The shining metal. So that was why Pettigrew set up for trading in the river canyon. I watched as the two white men made sign and the Utes returned sign. Back and forth. Arguing, pleading, cajoling perhaps.

I looked back at the cabin. There were rifle barrels sticking out of holes in the logs. The cabin was a miniature fort. Both of the white men wore pistols. I gathered that if there was trouble, the Pettigrews were prepared to defend themselves.

Finally, the Utes finished picking over the cooking utensils and signed that they would be back the next sun. The men waved to the Indians as they rode back across the river. Then Pettigrew and his helper packed up everything and put it back in the wagon, closed up the rear gate.

A woman the older man's age came out on the porch.

"Amos, supper's ready. You and Jasper wash up in the river."

The two men walked to the river and rolled up their sleeves.

No sign of Kate. I wondered if she sat down at the table with the family or if she had to eat scraps in their kitchen. The more I thought about her situation, the angrier I became.

I waited until the two men went inside the house. It was getting dark and I had to find a place to sleep. A place that was safe. Yet I didn't want to leave. Kate was inside that house and I wanted to watch over her. I realized how unrealistic that was. She didn't even know I was so close, and as for the Pettigrews, they had me outgunned. Maybe, I thought, after the Utes finished trading, they would pack up and leave. Then the Pettigrews would be alone. When Kate came to the river again to fill the buckets, perhaps I could call to her and we could slip away unnoticed.

I walked back to where I had left the horses. I rode downriver, keeping to the trees, then climbed a ridge and rode until I came to a plateau, a level place. I went across it and into the trees, started looking for a place to camp. I was going to unload the packhorse and put a bridle on it the next day. I would ride that horse and let Kate have the gelding with the saddle on its back.

I was tired, but that was no excuse for what I neglected to do. I was all jumpy inside at seeing Kate, and that too was no excuse for not scouting out my surroundings. I saw that grassy plateau and it looked like an oasis to me. I started to set up camp when I heard the click of a rifle bolt.

"Mister, you even twitch and I'll blow a hole in your back."

The voice surprised me as much as the warning. It was a woman's voice. I froze in my tracks, my left hand full of hobble rope.

"Don't shoot, ma'am. I mean you no harm."

"Maybe you can explain what you're doin' here on my property. Don't turn around. Just keep still."

"Are you goin' to shoot him, Ma?"

A tiny voice. I couldn't tell if it was a boy's or a girl's. It was definitely in the higher register of a very young voice.

"I'm just tired, ma'am. Looking for a place to sleep for the night."

"Tired? Mister, I saw you sneakin' up this canyon a long while back. I saw you when you came down to the ford and crossed the Poudre. I wondered what you were up to, and then I find you in my backyard. You aren't tired. You're up to no good and I want to know what it is you're looking for. My finger's getting awfully heavy on this trigger, so you better have some answers. Turn around so's I can take a look at you before it's plumb dark."

I turned around slowly.

The light was dim, but there was a beautiful young woman standing there. She couldn't have been more than sixteen or seventeen, from the looks of her freckle-peppered face and her curly russet hair that hung in ringlets over her tiny ears. Standing next to her was a little girl in a gingham dress who looked to be no more than four or five, with a precocious grin on her face and the same kind of hair in miniature. This woman must have married very young, or else that was her little sister standing next to her.

"You're wearing clothes that have hardly been broken in yet. What did you do, just get out of prison?"

"No, ma'am. I just escaped from the Arapaho a few days ago. I'm up here looking for my sister. She was kidnapped by the same tribe, but the Utes stole her and sold her to some Americans."

"Your sister?"

"Yes'm."

"What's your sister's name?"

There was something about her tone that gave me hope that she wasn't going to shoot me. She seemed genuinely curious. Not as suspicious.

"Kate, ma'am. Kate Sunnedon."

"What's your name?"

"Jared. Jared Sunnedon."

"You get your horses and come with me," she said. "I want to hear more of what you got to say. No funny moves now. I'm a crack shot and this is a Winchester repeating rifle with a full magazine."

She knew her stuff apparently.

"Yes'm. I know the rifle. I've got one just like it. Two, in fact."

"Just get moving. You aren't out of the woods yet, Mr. Sunnedon."

She said the name as if she was already used to it. I got my horses, led mine by the bridle, the packhorse by the lead rope. I followed the woman and the little girl across the meadow and through a fringe of trees. On the other side of the trees was a continuation of the same meadow and a log cabin sitting on the leading edge. I glanced left and could see the mountains on the other side of the river. From her front porch, she could have seen me riding down to the river. What a fool I was. I hadn't seen the cabin because it was hidden behind pine trees, but she sure as hell had a clear view of me when I came out on the other side of the river.

I put the horses up in a small stable she had on the other side of the house. There was a horse already in a stall. There was a small wagon parked alongside.

"Come on inside," she said, waving that rifle at me.

"Are you going to shoot him, Ma?" the little girl said.

"Never mind, Velma. You just go on inside and play with your little doll."

As we walked around the house, I noticed a storm cellar sunk into the earth. The door had a big padlock on it. I thought I heard something moving inside, but I didn't say anything.

We went into the front room, and she locked the door behind me.

"Sit in that chair over there," she said. Velma ran off into another room. I figured there were four rooms in the house, a front room, a kitchen, a bedroom or two.

I sat down.

"Let me see that hat," she said, sitting on the divan. "Just sail it over here to me."

I took off my hat and flipped it to her. She caught it with one hand.

"Where'd you get this hat?" she asked.

"It's a long story."

"I'm listening."

"How far back do you want me to go?"

"You can start with telling me how you and your sister got captured by Indians."

"That'll take quite awhile, ma'am."

"We've got all the time in the world. You're not going anywhere, and neither am I."

So I started with my life in Kansas City and told her the whole story, without mentioning any names. I told her of the killing of the two Indian boys and how we were driven from the wagon train and left on our own. I told her how my parents had been killed by the Arapaho.

She listened raptly to every word, but I got the feeling she had heard some of it before.

I told her about the two men who came gunning for me and how they killed the Cheyenne girl who was with me. I said I took their guns and such, packed them both down to La Porte.

"I kept the hat from one of the men I killed. It fit me better."

She looked at the hat in her lap, and tears began to seep from her eyes and flow down her cheeks. She grabbed the crown and squeezed it into a crumpled mass. Then she looked up at me.

"T-tell me," she said, "the names of the men you killed."

"Cassius Hogg and Rudy Truitt, ma'am. They were sure as hell trying to kill me. And the one named Rudy, he killed Blue Owl, who never hurt a fly."

"I knew he was no damned good," she said.

"Ma'am?"

She didn't say anything for several moments.

"Do you know the name of the man who has your sister?"

"Yes'm. Amos Pettigrew. He bought her from Hogg and Truitt, I figure, who traded with the Utes for them."

"Do you know what happened to the two little Indian girls the Utes stole when they captured your sister?"

"No, ma'am. I never heard what happened to them."

"Are you curious about that?"

"Why, yes, I am. I thought maybe they had been sold to somebody in Fort Collins."

She shook her head. She was still crying.

"Jared, I know your sister Kate. She told me much of the same story. My heart cries out for that girl. I wasn't much older than she is when I married Velma's father. I was fifteen. That man made my life miserable. He was never home much, and when he was, he was drunk. He beat me and treated me like dirt under his feet."

"I'm sorry to hear that, ma'am."

"Will you quit calling me 'ma'am' like I'm an old lady? My name is Rebecca Truitt. Rudy was my husband."

You could have knocked me down with a hummingbird feather when I heard that.

"In fact," she said, "my name is Rebecca Pettigrew Truitt. Amos is my father, and he's cut from the same bolt of cloth that Rudy was. They're both bastards."

I just sat there, stunned. The world I had fashioned in the past few days whirled and spun around, turned topsy-turvy, flew off into unfathomable space. Scrambling everything in it, turning me upside down, and emptying me out like an overturned pitcher of water.

And then I wondered when Rebecca Pettigrew Truitt was going to shoot me dead and hang my hide up on her living room wall.

Twenty-six

With the sun going down fast behind the high peaks, it was getting chilly inside the cabin. My nerves were shredded raw, like carrots my mother used to fix for boiling. Rebecca sat there with the rifle next to her, my hat in her lap, its crown wadded up like heavy paper. Her blue eyes glistened with tears, and she stared at me as if I was a man already condemned to death.

Then her eyes softened, and the tenseness went out of her face. Her shoulders relaxed and she drew in a deep breath. Her breasts pushed against the cloth of her simple, homespun dress, pert and perfect. She was a beautiful young woman who had just learned that her husband was dead and the man sitting in her front room had done the deed.

"I—I wasn't prepared for all this," she said, her voice soft as spun silk. "I—I'm trying my best to get over the shock."

"I'm sorry I killed your husband. I had to, or he would have killed me."

She shook her head.

"No, no, I understand that. I always thought Rudy was living on time borrowed from the devil. He was a wicked, wicked man, with no regard for the law or the rights and freedoms of others. I married him to get away from my family and I'm still trying to get away from them. I will get away from them someday if it's the last thing I do."

"Why are you living up here, so close to them?"

"Rudy and Cassius, with some help from my brother and my father, built this house for me. Before that, I stayed with my mother and father. I was miserable. When my father brought your sister Kate home, I stood it as long as I could. I told Rudy that I wanted a house of my own. I couldn't stand to see what my mother and father were doing to Kate. But I couldn't help her either. You must understand. Before Kate came, I was treated just like she was, or worse. So I moved here. This last winter was the most peaceful I've ever spent in my life."

"You stayed up here all winter?"

"Yes. You didn't see the cordwood outside? Have you seen my larder? You saw the springhouse."

"I thought it was a storm shelter."

She laughed.

"Not up here. There are no twisters. Just snow. Blessed, peaceful snow, all winter long. Velma and I enjoyed our time alone together. We played games, I taught her to sew and knit and how to boil water. It was a lovely time, Jared. Rudy was gone and I almost forgot he even existed. I dreaded the day he would come back and beat me in front of little Velma."

I said nothing. I couldn't imagine a young woman and a little girl spending a hard winter in the mountains, cut off from all human contact.

"Come," she said. "I want to show you something."

She got up, leaving the rifle on the divan. She handed me back my hat, but I dropped it on the chair. I looked past the chair at the back wall and saw a bookcase filled with books. I couldn't help myself. I walked over to it and began looking at the titles.

There was *Ivanhoe* and *The Count of Monte Cristo*, works by Shakespeare, Coleridge, and Dante, *The Vicar of Wakefield* and novels by James Fenimore Cooper, and many others. Seeing those books almost made me drunk.

"You read, Rebecca?"

"Yes. I read to Velma all winter, and I read myself to sleep at night."

"These are wonderful books. Mine were all burned up by the Utes."

"You must read some of mine. Come."

We walked into the hallway. Velma emerged from a bedroom.

"Mommy, it's dark."

"I know, sweetie," she said. "Mommy's going to light a lamp. Then, after a while, I'll fix us some supper."

Rebecca went into the dark room while I waited outside. I heard movements, then saw a flicker of light, after the scrape of a match. Light streamed through the doorway.

"Thank you, Mommy."

"You wait here. Mr. Sunnedon and I are going outside. We won't be long."

"Yes, Mommy."

I heard the sound of bed slats as the girl sat down on the bed. They creaked with her weight.

We walked to the kitchen, where Rebecca lit another lamp. She kept the match lit and in a little room just inside the back door, she lifted the chimney on a lantern and lit it.

She reached up to a shelf and took down a key, held it in her other hand. She walked outside and I followed her, wondering where she was taking me.

The sun was down and there was a furnace blazing just below the high mountain peaks. Small, salmon-hued clouds hung motionless in the afterglow, their bellies pulsating with the feeble saffron rays that slanted upward like the ribs of a Japanese fan. A stillness hung in the thin air like the hush before a storm. It was still light enough to see, and the lantern seemed incongruous in the eerie glow of dusk. The radiant sunset appeared destined to last forever as Rebecca made her way to the springhouse.

Then, as Rebecca reached the door of the springhouse and put the key to the lock, the clouds turned to ash and the colors in the sky paled to a dusky gauze and disappeared into a stygian darkness. The lantern sprayed us with golden light as the tumblers in the lock splayed open and the lock parted. She removed it and opened the twin doors, held the lantern high.

"Gray Dove," she said. "Spotted Fawn. Come out. Quick, quick."

Rebecca stepped back from the door, and two small red-skinned girls came out, their faces solemn with fear, their dark eyes gleaming like black agates in the lantern shine.

The girls looked at me. I smiled, recognizing them, even though they wore blue and white gingham dresses and little shoes and stockings.

I spoke to them in Arapaho, while Rebecca closed the two doors and reattached the lock, closed its curved bar with a dull click.

"Do you remember White Man?" I asked.

"Gray Dove remembers you, White Man. Did you come to take us home to our lodge?"

"No. I am hiding like you, like a little mouse. There are many Ota in the mountains."

Both girls giggled and put their hands over their mouths.

"Inside," Rebecca whispered to me, and we followed her back to the house, went in the back door, where she blew out the lantern and latched the door.

"Play with Velma," she told the girls, pointing to the bedroom where her own child lay on the bed with her doll, I imagined.

"You have taught them English."

"A few words. They are very bright. Like new pennies."

"How . . . ?"

"When I left my father's house, I took them with me. When he came up here after them, I told him I would kill him if he laid a hand on them."

"You would kill your own father?"

"To protect my girls, yes. I would kill my brother too. The girls were no more than house dogs to my folks, Jared."

"But your own flesh and blood . . ."

She struck a match and lit the kindling in the firebox of the small stove. The room became warm as she lit the main fire to the oven. She handed me a knife as she pulled a bowl of turnips and another of potatoes from a pantry below the kitchen counter. From another, she took a chunk of fresh meat.

"You cut up the vegetables," she said, "while I put a kettle on the stove."

The kettle was already full of water and sprinkled with spices. She set it on one of the griddles, then began cutting up the meat.

"Fresh venison," she said. "I shot a muley yesterday."

"What's a muley?"

"A mule deer. You know, the ones with big ears. They look like giant mice."

"I did not know they were called that."

"Well, they are."

"About your pa and brother . . . How could you even think . . . ?"

"Jared, there's no love lost between me and my parents, my no-account brother. They're evil people, every one of them. There's not an ounce of kindness in my mother, nor my father, and my brother is just plain mean, without any conscience whatsoever."

"But they're your kin, your own flesh and blood, Rebecca."

She turned to me, the knife poised in midair just above the venison. She compressed her lips in a tight rigor of anger. All of the softness vanished from her face as if it had been wiped hard with sandpaper, taking all the smoothness away, leaving a stark lined etching of an inner hatred.

"I don't know if people become bad, or if they are born bad. But my mother and father, I think, were born plumb bad. I've lived with their greedy, scheming, devious ways all my life. They never showed any love toward me or my brother, Jasper. But my brother took to their ways like a duck to water. He's a weak, spineless, heartless demon, just like they are. I loved my parents, despite their cruelty and deception, but when I saw what they were doing to your sister and those two little Indian girls, I vowed that I would fight them to the death before they'd harm another child. I wanted to take Kate with me too, but I couldn't fight all three of them. They would have killed us all, including Velma, and never batted an eye. That's how damned evil they are. I loathe the name Pettigrew and what it stands for. I loathe everything about these people, and no longer call any of them kin."

I sucked in a breath, shocked by Rebecca's revelation. I had never heard anything like it before, and her feelings were difficult to grasp. I could not imagine a child, a girl no less, turning against her parents. But I had no doubt her feelings were genuine.

"You know why I didn't shoot you when I first saw you, Jared? Do you know why I let you keep that pistol on your belt?"

"No. Why?"

"Because I recognized you from Kate's description, from that look of kindness on your face. I knew, in my heart, that you would come for her someday, and so did your sister. When she got that note from you, I noticed the change in her. And do you know what she said to me?"

"No."

"She said, 'Becky, my brother Jared always read to me of heroes. He is my hero. And he will come and rescue us both.'"

"Kate said that?"

"Yes, she did. You'd be surprised at what's inside the minds of children."

"I reckon so."

"Now, go out and get your rifles and bring them inside. I'll finish up the vegetables. And after supper, we're going to talk about how you can get your sister away from those evil people. I can't go with you, but I hope I can help you find a way to become her hero."

"You—you don't want me to kill your folks and your brother, do you? I don't know if I could do that."

"Jared, you will do what a hero would do. Your sister is in dire peril. If my brother or my father, or even my mother, knew you were here, that you wanted to take Kate away from them, they would shoot you dead and never shed a tear or have a twinge of conscience."

"But . . ."

"Go get your rifles. We're alone up here, Jared, and there are two dozen Utes camped right across the river from those damned Pettigrews. None of us here in this house are safe right now. So, git."

I walked out to the stable in the dark, stars gleaming like diamonds on black velvet. It seemed I could reach up and touch them, they were so close. I realized that I was on a strange journey, like Odysseus, like my hero.

And all about me, darkness and invisible gods.

Twenty-seven

It may not have been the best supper I ever had, but it ranked right up there at the top. I think the taste of the food was enhanced by being with a family, unusual as that family was, I admit. Becky knew how to cook venison and put a meal on in a hurry. While her pot was boiling, she seared the meat in a fry pan. When she put the venison in the water with the vegetables, she put the iron lid on, and when you put a fork in the meat, it just about melted before you could get it into your mouth.

Velma was a talky little girl, and she had those Arapaho girls giggling all through the meal. They had learned to communicate with each other somehow, and all three girls spoke a combination of English, Arapaho, and sign language, much to the delight of Becky and me.

"Vel, don't talk with your mouth full," Becky admonished her daughter. "You'll choke on your food."

Little Velma made the sign of talking, choking, and then acted it all out. Gray Dove and Spotted Fawn both mimicked her, until Becky's face turned red with embarrassment. But she didn't scold the girls for making fun of her. Instead, she said one word: "English."

All three little girls replied in chorus: "Yes, ma'am."

They sounded like baby birds cheeping.

I sat in the front room while Becky and the girls washed the dishes. I had brought one of my tablets in with my rifles, along with two pencils. I sharpened one and began to write. That was something I had done all my life before I went to bed, even when we all were in the wagon train, and sometimes when I was with One Dog.

The soft laughter coming from the kitchen was a soothing sound to me that evening, and it felt good to have a pencil in my hand again.

I was so absorbed in my writing I didn't hear Becky put the girls to bed, nor did she stir me when she entered the room.

"What are you writing?" she asked.

My whole body galvanized at the sound of her voice. I felt as if I had jumped inside my skin and it had stretched to the tautness of a drumhead.

"Just some thoughts."

"You should be thinking about Kate and how you're going to get her away from my father."

"I am thinking about Kate. Tomorrow, I'm going to scout the cabin down there and watch for Kate. When she comes to the river for water, I intend calling to her so she'll know I'm here. If there's a chance, we might be able to get away unnoticed."

Becky shook her head. "That woman watches her every minute."

"That woman?"

"Myrtle Pettigrew."

"Your mother, you mean."

"She's not my mother. Not my real mother."

"She's not?"

"My father murdered my mother. Myrtle is my step-mother."

"You don't mean your father actually . . . ?"

She sat across from my chair, at one end of the divan. She looked down at her hands, then back up at me.

"One night, when I was about five or six, there was a terrible row. I had been asleep. My brother and I woke up. We went out to the kitchen, but didn't go in. My father had my mother backed up against the wall and was beating her with his fists. There was blood coming out of her mouth, her nose, and her ears. She fell down and he kicked her until she stopped screaming. The next day, we buried her in the woods. This was back in Tennessee. My mother's name was Lorelei. She was only twenty-two when she died."

"What about your brother? Does he hate his father for what he did?"

"He fears him. He was possessed by the power in my father's fists. To this day, all my father has to do is raise his voice or clench his fist and my brother cowers like a cur dog and tucks his tail between his legs."

"I don't know what to say, Becky. I—I'm sorry. What a terrible thing for a child to witness."

"I fear my father too. He's a very dangerous man. You must be very careful if you go down there tomorrow. He won't hesitate to kill both you and Kate if he catches you trying to take her away from him. He's very possessive."

"If I can talk to Kate, maybe she can sneak out at night, after everybody's asleep."

"I've been in that cabin, Jared. The floors squeak. And

both Myrtle and my father have keen ears. It would be very difficult, if not impossible."

"Well, I'll think of something."

Becky laid out a bedroll for me in the front room. I had a hard time trying to go to sleep. I kept thinking of Kate being with those people and what Pettigrew had done to Becky's mother. When I did sleep, my dreams were filled with stark images of horror where I faced down a man and my guns melted and wouldn't shoot. The man had no recognizable human features, but his face was shaped like a giant ear and his fists were as big as hams, all covered with blood.

I left early before Becky and the girls were up. I rode the horse bareback and carried one of the rifles and plenty of ammunition. I hid the horse in the woods and walked to the same place I had been before, near the river. There was smoke above the lodges of the Utes, and the chimney of the cabin was streaming smoke as well.

I waited, well hidden, and watched both the Ute camp and the cabin.

Kate was the first to emerge from the cabin. She was carrying the yoke and two empty wooden pails, as before. She headed my way, went to the same spot as she had the night before. She was within earshot when she pulled the yoke from her shoulders and lifted one of the pails to dip it into the Poudre.

"Kate," I called, in a loud whisper. "Don't turn around. It's me, Jared."

She stiffened as she held the pail down and let the running water fill it.

"Kate. I've come to get you."

"Go away, Jared. Please."

"I'm staying with Rebecca."

She filled the pail and set it on the shore. She kept her head down, as if not daring to look in my direction.

"Can you get away from them tonight?"

She picked up the other pail and turned her back to me. She dipped it in the river. I could hear the water gurgling as it rushed against the pail.

"No, Jared. Stay away. Please."

"You've got to get away from Pettigrew. I'll be back this afternoon."

"They're watching me," she said.

"I know. Just come to this same place. I'll be waiting for you."

Myrtle came out onto the porch, looked downriver at Kate.

"Hurry it up, girl. What's taking you so damned long?" Myrtle's voice was loud and shrill.

"I'm coming," Kate shouted back.

"Look for me, Kate. I'll be here."

She finished filling the pail, set it next to the other one. Then she stood up, put the yoke over her shoulders, and lifted the pails by their ropes and put them in the grooves on either end.

She didn't look my way, nor did she reply. Myrtle was still on the porch, watching her every move. I felt like running over to Kate, knocking the yoke from her shoulders, snatching her up, and carrying her away.

Amos came out on the porch just then, and he too stood watching Kate. He had a rifle in his hands. Then his son Jasper joined him, and he also had a rifle. They were suspicious, I thought. And all three people on that porch were watching Kate like a hawk. She trudged off toward the cabin, her back bent under the weight of the yoke and

the water in the pails. I felt sorry for her. I fingered the trigger guard on my rifle. I'd have to shoot true and fast to
bring those men down, and then the Utes would probably
swoop down on me and Kate.

I ground my teeth and did nothing, except curse under
my breath.

I stayed there all day. The Utes crossed over with packhorses and traded with the Pettigrews all afternoon.

Kate did not come down to the river again that day. The
Utes packed up the goods they had bought, loading them
on travois, and crossed the river, rode up to their lodges.

Amos Pettigrew, after closing up his wagon, walked
downriver, stopped at the spot where Kate filled the pails.
He was carrying a Winchester and there was a Colt pistol
on his gun belt. He was so close I could hear him breathing.
He looked down at the water, then up at the mountains. He
studied Kate's tracks, then walked back to the cabin, apparently satisfied.

I breathed easier after he left. What had he been looking
for? Was he suspicious? He never once looked in my direction, or had I missed something?

I rode back to Becky's, discouraged.

For the next three days, I waited in the woods behind
that small ridge, but Kate never came down my way. But I
saw the Utes strike their lodges and vanish into the mountains. Jasper filled the water pails, closer to the cabin, a
couple of times, and Myrtle filled them once. But no Kate.
I began to worry, and on the fourth day of my vigil, I rode
around to the back of their cabin, tied my horse to a sturdy
pine, and walked down to look at the cabin from the rear.

There was a large shed to the left of the cabin, a lean-to,
and a pole corral where they kept the horses. It was out in

the open, unprotected, and I knew better than to inspect it up close.

There was an outhouse, a wooden privy covered with pine slabs. I saw Kate come out twice, Myrtle at her side. Jasper and Amos came out separately, one at a time. There was no back porch, just some rustic steps at the back door. I made my way back up the slope, got on my horse, and rode back to Becky's.

"They're watching Kate pretty close, Becky."

"I told you."

"I don't know what to do. Kate warned me away and I don't know why."

"She's trying to save her life and yours," Becky said.

"There has to be a way to get her out of there." I told Rebecca about the outhouse.

Becky shook her head. "Whenever Myrtle and Kate go out there, either Jasper or my father, or both, will be standing back of the window, watching. And they'll have rifles in their hands."

"Well, I'm going to get Kate away from them, Becky. If it's the last damned thing I do."

"It might be the last thing you do, Jared," she said.

"At least the Utes are gone. I don't have to worry about them."

"They'll all be going to town soon. You don't have much time. And in a few days, I'll have to take the wagon down and buy supplies."

I had a hunch.

"Does Kate ever go outside after dark to get water?" I asked Becky.

"Sometimes. Not often."

"What are people afraid of most?" I asked her.

"I don't know. What are you thinking?"

"Of ways to get all of them out of that cabin, including Kate."

"It could be dangerous," Becky said, as if reading my thoughts.

"It'll have to be light enough to see," I said.

"Yes. There's bound to be some shooting. At you."

"And me at them," I said.

"Do you plan to . . . ?"

"The privy," I said. "It'll burn fast and threaten the house. Maybe they'll rush out with those pails of water and leave their guns inside."

I knew what people were afraid of, and so did Becky.

Fire.

Twenty-eight

When the child of morning, rosy-fingered Dawn, appeared,
Odysseus put on his shirt and cloak. . . .

I thought of Homer's words as I dressed in the dark, knowing I was venturing into an unknown realm where human lives were at stake, including my own and my sister Kate's.

As I strapped on my pistol, Becky entered the front room.

"I've packed what you need, Jared. Some scraps of cloth, coal oil, and lucifers. I put them all in a flour sack and made a sling so that you can carry it on your shoulders."

"Thanks, Becky. Wish me luck?"

"I wish you Godspeed, Jared."

We spoke in whispers because the girls were still asleep. Her whisper had a kind of sleepy husk to it that stirred my blood, seeped into my manhood like delicate female fingers. A whisper that touched the deepest parts of me and made me feel embarrassed at my carnal thoughts. I was nervous too, but tried not to show it. I picked up my rifle and we walked out into the kitchen. There, on the counter, was the sack with the fire-making materials. She had slit the large sack and tied two pieces together to make a sling. I put it on my shoulder, tested it. The knot was strong and the sack rested just beneath my left armpit.

"It works, Becky."

"Here, put these lucifers in your pocket."

I took the matches and put them in my shirt pocket. Our fingers touched, briefly but lingeringly, and there was that odd feeling again, a rush of warmth to my loins, a yearning in me that was deeper than anything I had ever felt before, a feeling that a man has for a woman when she is in season.

"Be seeing you," I said lightly, but realized that my voice had a quaver in it. At least my hands were not shaking. Not yet.

I looked deep into her eyes at that moment, into those smoky blue eyes, and felt something inside me falling, floating downward from a great height. It was a moment of knowing between us, a solemn, sacred knowing, as if a godlike voice was calling to both of us, bidding me to stay, urging her to hold onto my fingers a while longer and draw me into her, into those secret depths of her where all was quiet and peaceful and grander than anything on earth. The moment lasted an eternity and I saw, for an instant, that divine spark of lust that flares up when a woman wants a man, wants him almost desperately and forever.

She didn't speak, and I realized that Becky was as scared as I was. But of what? Of wanting me, or of just letting me go into that deepest, darkest cave where dragons lurk and heroes die before their time? I would lose the concealment of darkness if I tarried, so I broke the gaze and turned my back on a woman glowing with an earthy desire.

I slipped out the door and went to my horse, which I had tied up out back earlier that morning. Again, I rode bareback through the pines over a now-familiar trail.

There was just a smear of cream in the eastern sky, barely visible over the jumble of foothills. I could see my breath in the chill morning air, and I was shivering when I dismounted, whether from fear or the cold, I did not know.

Becky had wrapped the bottles of coal oil in the rags so they didn't clink as I walked down the slope of the small ridge to the back of the outhouse. I was careful not to make any noise, but it was precarious going with movable stones underfoot, brush, tree branches, and small fissures eroded by flowing water. There were no lamps lit in the cabin, at least no lights that I could see. I crouched down behind the small building and slowly eased the sling off my shoulder. I laid my rifle down beside me. There was a cartridge in the chamber and the hammer was pulled back to half-cock. My Colt was fully loaded with six cartridges. I had slid the cylinder so that the hammer rested on the metal between bullet chambers. The Colt was a single-action, so I'd have to cock the hammer back to lock the cylinder into place and be able to fire it.

I clumped the rags together and pulled the cork on one of the bottles. I soaked the rags with coal oil, making sure they were each saturated. I placed these around the base of the outhouse on three sides. I stuffed a rag in an open knothole. Then I doused the entire back of the building with oil, splashing it on gently so that I didn't make any noise. I set the empty bottle right against the baseboard of the wooden structure. I picked up my rifle and laid down a line of coal oil from the building, crab-walking backward. I hoped all of it would not seep into the ground and fail to ignite.

I made sure that the outbuilding concealed me from view, and piled up brittle pinecones and needles, then soaked that with the last of the coal oil. I set the bottle down, out of the way, and walked to a hiding place I had chosen that gave me a full view of the cabin, the back steps, and the outhouse. There, rifle at the ready, I waited for the sky to pale.

I took out the matchbox. There was a strip of sandpaper glued to its side that had never been used. The box and the sandpaper were dry, and I intended to keep them that way. The brand name on the box read LUCIFER, and depicted a red devil with horns on its head and a horned tail. I took one of the matches out. It would take me three strides to get to the pile of oil-soaked pinecones and needles. I only had to wait for the first early riser to enter the outhouse. I hoped like hell it wasn't Kate.

Sunlight began to flow up the canyon, splashing color onto the bluffs, tinting the boulders, burning green on the pinos. The cold from the ground rose up in a shivering chill as the earth began to warm. In one of the windows of the cabin, I saw a glow as someone inside lighted a lamp. I stared until my eyes watered trying to see who had done this, but saw only a play of light and shadows beyond the pane.

I heard a soft click in my ear and sensed a presence next to me. A hand reached down and grabbed the box of matches.

"I'll take those," a voice said. "Kids shouldn't play with matches."

I turned slowly and looked up as the man hurled the box to the ground. Jasper Pettigrew stood there, a cocked Colt in his hand. I was looking straight down the pistol's black snout.

"I saw your tracks yesterday, sonny. I been waitin' for you. Now you just get up real slow and leave that rifle where it lays."

I acted as if I was going to get up and let Jasper kill me. He was just too sure of himself. As I got my feet under me, I reached out, grabbed the barrel of his pistol, and jerked him down on top of me. I slid my finger up the barrel and stuck it between the hammer and the cartridge primer. With my right hand, I slammed a fist into his throat, hoping to crack his vocal chords so that he could not cry out.

I felt small bones crunch under my fist. Jasper made a gurgling, croaking sound in his throat as I snatched his pistol out of his hand. We rolled a foot or two and he began clawing at my face, trying to gouge out my eyes. I dropped the pistol, throwing up my arm to defend myself. He jabbed a thumb in my left eye. I knocked his hand away and scrambled to get on top of him. He squirmed like a snake to avoid getting pinned. I grabbed his throat with my right hand and squeezed as hard as I could. He shook his head and his body convulsed as he tucked his legs up and tried to roll out from under me.

His breathing came hard and raspy, but he was still strong, sinewy, with flexing muscles that rippled under the skin of his arms. He slammed me in the temple with a solid haymaker right, and stars danced in my brain like tiny moths caught in a searing light.

He reached down and drew a knife as we rolled back and forth. He tried to jab me with the blade, but I grabbed his wrist and forced his arm to the ground. I bore down hard and his fingers came apart. The knife slid from his grasp. I brought a knee up and kicked him square in the groin. He gasped and doubled over in pain. We both looked at the knife lying there. He went for it, but I was faster.

I snatched up the knife and Jasper's eyes went wide. He opened his mouth to scream and pushed on my chest with both arms. I drove the knife downward, slicing his arm before I plunged it into his throat. Blood bubbled up and sprayed my face in a sudden burst. Jasper quivered all over like a beheaded chicken, his legs flopping out of control.

"You bastard," I hissed, and slashed the blade across his throat until he lay still. My hand was bloody and I wiped it on his shirt. I rose up, panting from the exertion, and looked over at the house. The window was still glowing a pale orange and the sunlight was crawling up the logs.

Frantically, I picked up my rifle and retrieved the box of matches. I dashed to the pile I had made, and with trembling hands, I took out another match and raked it across the sandpaper strip.

The head of the match popped off and it didn't light. I struck another one and the phosphorus flared into flame. I touched the match to the soaked debris. And waited an eternity.

The fire caught, slowly, and began to flow along the path of coal oil I had made. So slowly did the fire creep, my heart started to pound in my temples. I lit another match, and it blew out before I could toss it onto the ground.

I ran back to where Jasper lay spread-eagled on the ground, his blood no longer pumping. Smoke rose from behind the outhouse and I saw the back door open. Myrtle came out and stood on the steps, then opened her mouth to scream.

"Amos!" she screeched.

It seemed that the fire took forever to reach the back of the outhouse, but once it did, the whole back wall erupted in flames. Myrtle went back inside the house and emerged a moment later, a bucket in her hand.

And right behind her was Kate, carrying another wooden pail.

The outhouse, with its dry old wood, burst into full flame, painting Myrtle a bright orange as she lifted the pail to hurl the water from it. She jumped back, and the water sloshed harmlessly onto the ground. Myrtle turned toward Kate, dropping her pail. She snatched the pail from Kate's hands and splashed water onto the fire. It was like throwing sand at a wall. The water turned to steam, evaporated in a hissing puff.

"Get more water," Myrtle screamed, throwing the empty bucket toward Kate.

Kate stooped over to pick up both buckets. She snatched them up by their rope handles and started to run toward me, around the side of the house. She dashed toward the river as Amos stepped outside, still wearing his long underwear, a Winchester in his hand.

"Pettigrew," I yelled. "You looking for Jasper? Here he is."

Myrtle turned toward me.

So did Amos. He swung around toward me, his rifle at hip level. I brought my own rifle up quick and thumbed the hammer back to full cock.

Amos fired first. His shot went wild, sizzling past my ear like a buzzing hornet. I dropped the sight on his mid-section and squeezed the trigger. The bullet caught him in the abdomen, spun him around. He staggered back on the landing and struck the back door.

Myrtle ran to him and pulled the rifle from his hand. She turned toward me, levering another cartridge into the firing chamber.

"Drop it," I said as I jacked another shell from the magazine. "Drop the rifle or I'll shoot you where you stand."

"Shoot him," Amos groaned.

I took direct aim at Myrtle Pettigrew, my finger just ticking the trigger.

The gas from inside the outhouse exploded, hurling pieces of wood, shit, piss, siding in all directions. Flaming fagots landed at Myrtle's feet and on the porch where Amos stood.

Myrtle screamed. Amos staggered down the steps and grabbed the rifle from her. He swung it in my direction. I fired, aiming for his heart. Myrtle started running toward me, infuriated, perhaps confused. Amos fired his rifle while his wife was directly in the line of fire. The bullet struck her in the back and she pitched forward, a big hole in her chest.

I squeezed the trigger as Myrtle struck the ground. My aim was off and the lead projectile hit Amos in the belly. He doubled over in pain, stared at me with a look of shock and rage. I worked the lever and slid another cartridge into the chamber.

Amos took two steps toward me, then collapsed. Blood soaked the ground beneath him as he gasped for breath.

The outhouse collapsed, what was left of it, sending a shower of sparks into the air.

I walked over to Amos and kicked the rifle out of his hand, away from his reach.

He looked up at me, his eyes rheumy with pain.

"Who—who are you?" he gasped.

"For you, Pettigrew," I said, "it's Sundown."

"Sundown," he said with his last breath, as if the word was a puzzle he would never figure out.

I walked down to the river where Kate was filling the wooden pails.

"Kate, it's over," I said. "You don't need to fill another bucket for those folks."

She turned and looked at me in bewilderment. She looked like a frightened fawn. Her eyes were wide and her lips quivered in fear.

"Jared?"

"Yes. Come, Kate. We'll ride up to Becky's and start all over."

"I—I'm not a prisoner anymore?"

"No. Never again."

I took my sister in my arms and held her tightly until her trembling stopped. We did not go near the house. I didn't want her to see what I had done. On the ride to Becky's, she came out of her stupor and began to talk.

"I was scared they might kill you if you came after me, Jared. I wanted to run away with you."

"I know. It's over now."

"Do you like Rebecca? She was the only one who was nice to me."

"Yes. She's a nice woman."

"She's pretty too."

"Yes. She is pretty. Very pretty."

"Did you—did you kill her father and her brother?"

"Yes."

"Are you going to tell her?"

"I think she already knows, Kate."

"You like her, don't you, Jared?"

"Yes. I like Becky a lot."

She squeezed me with her arms. I patted her hand.

"Good," she said with a sigh.

The sun cleared the foothills and showered us with golden warmth. There was a fresh scent to the pines that had been laden with dew. It felt good to have my little sister sitting behind me on horseback, free, finally. We had been on a long journey, she and I, and now we were heading for a place that looked like home.

And maybe, I thought, it would be our home.

Someday.

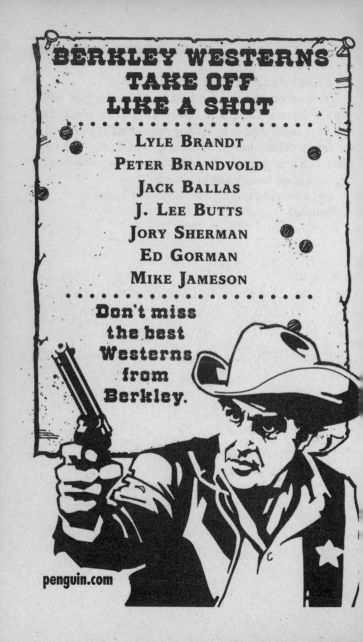